W9-BUC-611

BRONZE
DRAGON CODEX

R.D. Henham

MIRRORSTONE

Bronze Dragon Codex
©2008 Wizards of the Coast, Inc.

All characters in this book are fictitious. Any resemblance to actual persons, living or dead, is purely coincidental.

This book is protected under the copyright laws of the United States of America. Any reproduction or unauthorized use of the material or artwork contained herein is prohibited without the express written permission of Wizards of the Coast, Inc.

Published by Wizards of the Coast, Inc. MIRRORSTONE and its respective logo are trademarks of Wizards of the Coast, Inc., in the U.S.A. and other countries.

All characters, character names, and the distinctive likenesses thereof are property of Wizards of the Coast, Inc.

Printed in the U.S.A.

The sale of this book without its cover has not been authorized by the publisher. If you purchased this book without a cover, you should be aware that neither the author nor the publisher has received payment for this "stripped book."

Text by R.D. Henham with assistance from Amie Rose Rotruck
Cover art by Vinod Rams
Interior art by Todd Lockwood
Cartography by Dennis Kauth
First Printing: June 2008

9 8 7 6 5 4 3 2

Library of Congress Cataloging-in-Publication Data

Henham, R. D.
  Bronze dragon codex / R.D. Henham.
    p. cm.
  "Text by R.D. Henham with assistance from Amie Rose
Rotruck"--Copyright p.
  Summary: When Simle--a bronze dragon who hates humans--and Tatelyn--a
human who distrusts dragons--are linked sympathetically by a pendent,
they realize they must work together which brings them a better
understanding of each other.
  ISBN 978-0-7869-4930-4
  [1. Dragons--Fiction. 2. Magic--Fiction. 3. Cooperativeness--Fiction.
4. Fantasy.] I. Title.
  PZ7.H3884Br 2008
  [Fic]--dc22
                                                    2008003701

ISBN-13: 978-0-7869-4930-4
620-21824720-001-EN

U.S., CANADA,
ASIA, PACIFIC, & LATIN AMERICA
Wizards of the Coast, Inc.
P.O. Box 707
Renton, WA 98057-0707
+1-800-324-6496

EUROPEAN HEADQUARTERS
Hasbro UK Ltd
Caswell Way
Newport, Gwent NP9 0YH
GREAT BRITAIN
Save this address for your records.

Visit our web site at www.mirrorstonebooks.com

For Salem.

You were with me when I began this journey,

but unable to finish with me.

Happy running, dear friend!

—A.R.R.

To all those who seek friendship with dragons.

—R.D.H.

Dear Honored Scribe Henham,

Good day! I hope my last set of notes helped with your dragon research. I couldn't read what you said in the letter I was just handed, since it was positively caked in mud. (Your messenger caught me as I was digging beneath a black dragon's lair—more about him next time!) My guess is that you were delighted to hear from me, and want to hear more about Krynn's dragons!

I recently ran into my friend Tatelyn, whom I met while fighting the Dragon Queen Asvoria. After Asvoria possessed the body of a good copper dragon, she destroyed everything in her way—including Tatelyn's hometown.

Asvoria killed Tatelyn's brother, and in her despair Tatelyn vowed to rid Krynn of all dragons—even the good ones! That is, until a bronze dragon named Simle entered Tatelyn's life—a Bronze whose past had clouded her judgment about humans just as Tatelyn's past had clouded her view of dragons.

As before, I've attached my notes. (Please excuse the smudges. The black dragon is currently thumping about above our heads.) They detail the events that brought Tatelyn and Simle together, and the mysterious ancient jewels that made both of their lives more difficult (and exciting!). Not to mention the—

Oh, that was a wonderfully loud roar! I suppose I should hand this letter off to your messenger before we all become a dragon's supper. As interesting as that might be, my companions don't seem too keen on the idea. Until next time, Scribe Henham!

All my best,
Sindri Suncatcher
Noted Expert on the Arts of Wandering, Wild Sorcery, Interesting Tales, Dragon Studies, and (soon) Wizardry

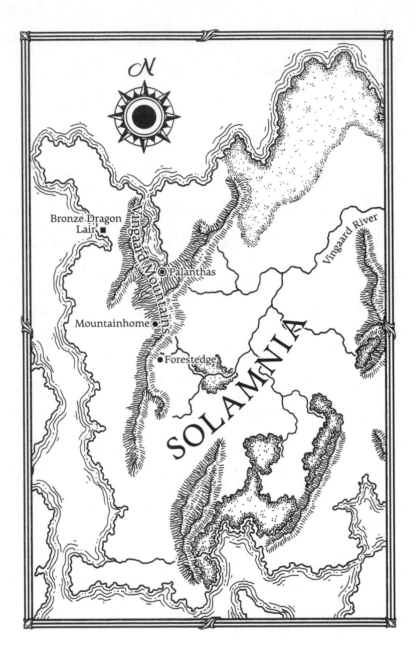

PROLOGUE

287 AC

Simle never was sure what woke her that day. One moment she was deeply asleep, as were her parents and, indeed, all the good dragons on Krynn, and the next moment she was suddenly awake. Banished thousands of years ago, the good dragons passed most of their time in slumber. But Simle was suddenly awake and instantly bored.

Simle stretched and yawned. A small bolt of lightning shot from her mouth and struck the sandy floor harmlessly. Simle jumped, both surprised and pleased. She had never used lightning before and she couldn't wait to do it again. Stretching her neck, Simle opened her mouth, but no lightning came. She pouted, wanting to show off her new trick to someone. Shooting lightning randomly—it would take many more years for her to learn to control it—meant she was almost big enough to learn to swim. If anyone ever woke up.

Her parents lay coiled a few feet away. Dragging her thin tail through the damp sand, Simle padded over to them, then stood up on her hind legs to look closer. In slumber, they both looked as though they had been delicately molded out of bronze. Her mother's horns were not quite as long as her father's, and there was a delicacy to her neck frill that Simle's father's lacked. But other than that, the two were like twin statues, their only movements the rise of their massive chests in sleep and, every once in a while, the flicker of a purple-gray tongue as one or the other let out a particularly rough breath.

"Mother? Father?" Simle tapped each parent lightly on the head. Neither of them budged. Simle sighed. This wasn't the first time she'd awoken while everyone else snoozed. They rarely woke when she tried to rouse them, and the one time she succeeded, they gave her such a tongue-lashing that she wasn't sure it was such a good idea to try again.

So instead she wandered to the next chamber where her siblings still slumbered. The tide came in regularly here, washing over the eggs and keeping them healthy. Unlike Simle's egg, which had hatched early—her father liked to tease her that she couldn't wait to enter the world—the other five eggs remained unhatched. They glittered there as if sunlight shone on them. She tipped her head, pondering the huge bronze orbs. Perhaps all they needed was a little encouragement. Simle nudged one with her nose. The egg rocked backward slightly, then forward to tap her forehead. Simle giggled and raised a tiny claw to tap it back.

Clatter. Scrape.

Simle whirled about, her claw still raised in the air. There it was again, a far-off sound that was not the waves at the cave entrance. A quick glance showed her parents still slept deeply. What was it? Simle cocked her head and then gasped. Voices in the cavern! Simle had never seen any living creature other than her parents and Uncle Nuvar, who slept in the next cave over. She knew there had to be more dragons around, and all sorts of animals roamed the Dragon Isles.

Simle considered waking her parents. She decided against that as she set off down the path that led to the ocean. She would see who those beings were, then bring them to her parents. As Simle walked down the sandy corridor, the voices became louder. She hid behind a rock to get a look at the visitors.

"Why did they send us to this sauna?"

Simle frowned. It wasn't an animal, and whoever it was didn't even speak Draconic. Simle didn't recognize the language, but her mother had told her that dragons could understand any creature on Krynn. This would be something entirely new, something she'd never seen before. Simle peeked around the rock.

Though total darkness engulfed this part of the cave, Simle's vision was better than most creatures'. She saw two figures, both standing on two legs and not much taller than her, although considerably thinner through the torso. No horns or scales. Their faces and forelimbs looked like the inside of shrimp. Shrimp-things, Simle silently dubbed them, though if they were shrimp, they were giant ones.

"I curse the day we drew this mission," the shrimp-thing who had spoken before said, his whisper breaking the silence like a whip crack. His companion clamped a firm hand over his mouth and whispered, "*Shirak.*" The faintest glow of light surrounded them like a halo. Now Simle could see that the lumps she'd taken to be the shrimp-things' bodies were animal skins draped over their forms. No wonder, Simle sniffed, looking at their pink faces and hands. Without scales, they would need protection.

The first shrimp-thing carried a long, sharp tooth tied to his waist, as well as a stringed arc and a round leather container filled with sticks. The other was smaller, with longer fur growing from her head. It had a more delicate look to it, so Simle thought they must be male and female, like her parents. Numerous pouches hung from the female's belt. Simle could smell all sorts of disgusting and appealing scents emanating from the pouches.

The shrimp-things stood silent for a moment, listening. The far-off sound of even, restful breathing echoed through the caves, accenting the rhythm of the waves.

"A trip to this infernal cave better be worth it, Milam," the male grumbled in a low voice, then coughed into one hand. "I can barely breathe for all the salt." While the air had a touch of moisture and even more of a taste of salt, it was a comfortable humidity. Simle took a few deep breaths. The air seemed fine to her. What was air like where these beings came from?

"If your delicate constitution can bear some heat and salt, Juru, you will find that this trip is indeed well worth it," the female said. Milam, the male had called her. A low rumble echoed through the cavern. Milam's green eyes widened. With a motion of one slender hand, she extinguished the faint light.

"You must trust me," she told Juru. "I can guide us." Juru placed one hand on Milam's shoulder and followed in her footsteps, heading straight to Simle.

Simle ducked back into the shadows, suddenly shy. What would she say to these creatures? They walked past her, not noticing the bronze dragon wyrmling whose eyes followed their every move. Once they were a bit ahead of her, Simle shadowed the two shrimp-things.

The farther they traveled, the louder the sighs of Simle's parents grew and the more the air around them stirred. A particularly noisy sigh, almost a huff, lifted the shrimp-things' head-fur in ripples.

"What is this place?" Juru looked in the direction of the loudest breathing and gasped. He stood face-to-face with Simle's father.

The dragon's head, resting on the floor, was fully as

tall as Juru. The eyes, large as melons, were closed in sleep. If Simle's father were to open his eyes, he could crunch his teeth around Juru as easily as a smaller creature eating a berry. Juru backed away, stumbled over a rock, and fell. Looking around wildly, he spotted Simle's mother behind him. He sank to the floor, unable to do anything but look back and forth between the two slumbering dragons.

Milam walked to Juru and put her hands on his shoulders, steadying him. "Yes," she whispered. "They do exist. But they do not concern us."

"Of course we exist!" Simle exclaimed, bounding over to the two shrimp-things. They both swung toward Simle, Juru drawing the long metal tooth and pointing it at her, and Milam reaching a hand into her pouch. Simle skidded to a halt in front of them. "I'm Simle, and those are my parents. Who are you? Did you come to visit us?"

Milam put one hand on Juru's arm, making him lower the sword. Her eyes went from Simle, to her parents, and to the chamber beyond, then back to Simle. They narrowed slightly.

"I am Milam, little wyrmling." Milam held up one hand that slightly shook. Simle flicked it with her tongue, and Milam seemed to relax. "Are you alone here?"

"My parents are asleep," Simle said, sniffing Juru. He smelled strange, almost like rotten fish. "My siblings are still in their eggs and won't come out to play." Simle looked at Milam hopefully. "Will you play with me?"

"Of course, little one," Milam said, scooping a rock the size of her fist from the ground. "But first, can you answer me this? How many siblings do you have?"

"Five," Simle said. She was very proud of her counting skills.

"Very good, wyrmling!" Milam looked at the rock in her hands and murmured, *"Khalayan."* The plain rock shimmered and became a glittering diamond. Simle gasped in delight as the large diamond bounced toward her and rolled to a stop at her feet. Never had Simle seen a gem so sparkly and pretty. Simle batted the diamond with one claw and it flew across the cave in a twinkling arc. She clambered after it, swiped her tail at it, and the diamond flew even farther.

Simle smiled, revealing rows of delicately pointed teeth. Simle's parents often allowed her to play with their treasure, but their taste ran to coral and gold, not glittering gems like this diamond. Milam was nice! Simle wasn't sure about Juru, but someone who would give her something so pretty was surely a friend.

Simle wasn't sure how long she played with the diamond. She became lost in the glittering clear depths of her toy, which was so like water on the brightest days. She followed the diamond through the cave, batting it farther and farther.

Suddenly, an anguished wail echoed through the cave. Simle jerked up from the diamond. Why was she here, so far from the nest? Simle took the diamond in her mouth and ran back her parents. As she ran, more howls echoed through the cave, shaking rock loose from the ceiling.

When Simle reached the main part of their cave, she skidded to a halt and thumped into her mother's flank. Her mother whirled to face her, inhaling sharply. When she focused her blazing bronze eyes upon Simle, she sobbed.

"Simle!" her father said, reaching down to cradle her with both front paws. "Where were you? We thought something terrible happened to you!"

"I was chasing this," Simle said, dropping the diamond at her parents' feet.

"A rock? You left the nest for a rock?" her mother choked.

"Not just a rock!" Simle said. "See how sparkly it—" Simle lost all words as she looked upon the object she'd dropped from her mouth. It was no longer a diamond with thousands of glittering facets. Simle had been chasing a rock exactly like the millions of rocks in the cave.

"But I'm here," Simle said. "I heard you crying. I'm here."

"And we're so glad you're safe," her father said, holding her tighter. "But something terrible has happened." Simle's father moved so Simle could look into the egg chamber.

Simle gasped, and the tiniest bolt of lightning shot from her mouth to strike harmlessly on the sandy floor.

The eggs were gone. All five of the wondrous, shimmering, bronze eggs had been taken.

"What happened?" Simle said in a small voice. "Did you move them?" she asked, clinging to one small hope.

Simle's mother shook her head. "They were stolen. Judging by the smell, I say by humans."

"Humans? I only saw—" Simle began, then her mother picked her up and forced her to look in her eyes. Simle told about the shrimp-things and the diamond, and her parents began to wail. They could not speak, but Simle knew. Milam and Juru had stolen her siblings. They were not friends at all. They were evil.

Simle curled into a ball against her mother and father. The three of them stood there, weeping tears that hissed and crackled on the sandy niche that once served as the nest. Simle cried until she could cry no more and fell asleep, exhausted. Two words in the tongue of dragons resounded in her brain as though burned there by a brand: *Dartak munthrek.*

I hate humans.

Chapter One

356 AC

"We must banish the dragons from Krynn!"

Tatelyn paused here, as she always did, and waited for her audience to react. Her age and small, slender stature often puzzled people when she took a podium. But if there was one thing Tatelyn had learned to do well in the past year, it was capture an audience with the power of her words.

This was the crucial moment, Tatelyn knew, from giving this same speech dozens of places. Either people began to look at her with agreement and interest, or they rolled their eyes and dismissed her as a lunatic. This time, though, the audience was different. This time, she stood in an amphitheater addressing a crowd of well-to-do city people, not country folk like herself. These knights and merchants were all citizens of Palanthas. Their beloved city was saved from destruction during the War of the Lance by the good dragons.

Or so they said. Tatelyn knew that there was no such thing as a good dragon.

She had taken special care to look as noble as she could so they couldn't hold her appearance against her, twining her hair into dozens of intricate black braids that wove around her head and cascaded down her back. She couldn't do anything about her plain blue cleric's robes, but she hoped her words could convince this audience where her clothes could not. The heat of the summer sun didn't help her appearance any, though, and she wasn't just sweating because of the heat. She *had* to convince these people. Their good opinion would make or break the Heirs of Huma in Palanthas.

There were some murmurs and darkened glances from some in the audience, but at least they were still listening. Tatelyn took a deep breath and continued, "My brother was cruelly murdered by a dragon. He did not die at the hands of the Dark Queen's minions, the chromatic dragons. My brother was killed by a copper dragon, one of the metallic dragons that dare call themselves 'good' dragons."

More people were muttering now, and they did not sound convinced. Tatelyn glanced to the front row where her friends sat, looking for their take on the crowd. They made a rather unusual rainbow: Rogan in his white and silver knight's armor, his sister Ramma in a brocaded white dress that was closer to a fine lady's gown than wizard robes. Combined with their brilliant clothing, the siblings' golden hair and lightly freckled skin made a curiously matched set with Elrit's toffee-colored skin and nondescript sailor's garb.

Rogan and Ramma had grown up in Palanthas and knew these people better than Tatelyn did. Both of them looked concerned, but Ramma motioned for Tatelyn to continue.

"How can creatures capable of such destruction be good? Their strength and magical capabilities are beyond what any human can ever hope to achieve. Without their eggs, those foul beasts known as draconians would never walk these lands."

At that last point, Tatelyn saw a few nods in the crowd. Palanthas knew how evil the draconians were. But there wasn't as high a percentage of people with open, curious faces as she was used to, not by a long shot. She was losing them. Better turn it over to Rogan. He might have better luck. Tatelyn launched into the conclusion of her speech. "I say that we were better off before these monsters returned to Krynn. Now that the war is over, we must devote our energies to one purpose. Those of us who pursue this purpose call ourselves the Heirs of Huma. We took this name because we seek to do what the hero Huma did once." Tatelyn took a deep breath and raised her voice high. "We must banish all dragons from Krynn!"

The crowd rose to its feet at this proclamation, which was normal. What was *not* normal was the fury in people's eyes, the clenched fists. Tatelyn's friends leaped to their feet and moved toward her. Elrit was first to reach the podium. The amphitheater erupted in derisive shouts.

"Forget it," Elrit said, grabbing Tatelyn by the arm. "We have to get out of here! You may have started a riot!"

"By talking?" Tatelyn pulled against Elrit. "We have to convince them! These are some of the most influential people with the Whitestone Council!"

"Tatelyn, these people won't be convinced!" Ramma grabbed Tatelyn's other arm, pulling her away from the audience, which was crowding down toward the podium. "I don't think they'll hurt you, but you could be imprisoned! For many knights, what you say is the same as treason."

"But none of you have had the chance to speak," Tatelyn insisted as Elrit pulled aside the backdrop behind the podium. "Rogan and Ramma, you have to tell them about how the dragons have destroyed the knighthood. And Elrit, you need to tell them about the silver dragon that killed your parents—"

"You think that would convince them?" Elrit asked, shoving Tatelyn through the curtain just in time to avoid a rotten tomato to the head. "I know a place where we can be safe until we can leave the city. Follow me!"

The air had been hot outside, but behind the curtain it was stifling and unbearable. They breathed gulps of fresh air when they popped out behind the forum. No one was here, but they could still hear the angry roar of the crowd.

"We should leave Palanthas now," Rogan said. "After that reaction, I don't think Ramma and I can protect you, even with the help of our influential friends."

"Protect her?" Ramma scoffed. "We'll probably be jailed ourselves!"

"I can't leave yet," Tatelyn said, leaning against a wall and feeling the warmth of the sun-heated bricks through her robe. "I wish we could see the Lady Crysania. Or Revered Son Elistan. If we could get the backing of the church, we might have a chance with the Whitestone Council."

"Lady Crysania isn't here. And besides, we can't march up to the temple now," Ramma argued. "People will notice you."

"Only the rich people at that meeting will notice her," Elrit corrected. "There's more to Palanthas than knights and merchants, though I don't suppose you and your brother ever really paid attention to that."

Ramma glowered at Elrit, but followed him as he led them to one of the worst parts of town. Ironically, it was directly behind the new temple of Paladine.

Although the wretched masses behind the temple wouldn't accost a cleric, they made Tatelyn nervous. She came from a mountain village, and while there had been hard winters and summer droughts, no one had ever starved or lacked a place to sleep. Here, though, in the richest city on Krynn, people slept in doorways, under rude tents made of cast-off lumber and filthy blankets, and on the street itself.

"Is this safe?" Ramma asked, hiding behind Rogan to avoid the reach of an old woman in rags.

Elrit sneered at her. "You and your family live like kings, yet pay no attention to the suffering right here at your feet. And you call my people barbarians." He walked away before Ramma could retort.

Looking ashamed, Ramma dug in her pockets for a few coins. The small pieces of steel Ramma was handing out were but a fraction of the girl's fortune. Elrit joined Rogan down the alley. He shook the hand of a mother holding a crying baby—or at least, Tatelyn thought he was shaking her hand, but when Elrit turned away, she broke a piece of bread and handed a portion to a small child clinging to her dress. He was handing out the food from his traveling pack.

With a sigh, Tatelyn looked up at the broad expanse of the back wall of the temple. It was so different on this side. If she closed her eyes, she could remember the first time she saw it, when she took her vows as an acolyte of Mishakal. To Tatelyn, the sight of the new temple at

Palanthas had been as welcome as fresh water and hot food after the long journey from Forestedge, her small hometown in the mountains.

Compared to the war-ravaged countryside of the Vingaard Mountains, the city had appeared as a gem set into a rough seam of rock. The beauty of the city paled next to the newly built temple of Paladine. A building constructed almost entirely of white marble could easily have appeared cold and foreboding, but the lush groves and gardens surrounding it, as well as the friendly faces of the clerics that moved about the grounds, made it warm and inviting.

But in the alleys behind the temple grounds, the scene was not so well groomed. Here, the destitute awaited the benevolence of passersby, begging for healing or food. Today there had to be at least thirty people on this one street alone in various states of sickness and desperation.

"Excuse me, miss?" said a young girl no older than Tatelyn. Her dress was more holes than cloth, and so filthy that Tatelyn was sure it would fall apart with one washing.

"Can I help you?" Tatelyn asked, straightening up. "Do you need to be healed?"

"No, I'm well for now, thank you kindly," the girl said. She clutched a gray shawl around her that reminded Tatelyn more of a fishnet. "Are you the one they speak of in the marketplace? The one who wants to banish the good dragons?"

Tatelyn opened her mouth to confirm, but Elrit caught her eye and shook his head slightly. Could it be a trap? Tatelyn looked around and saw that no one else was watching them. Either they were still pestering Rogan and Ramma for steel or accepting Elrit's food gratefully.

"I am," Tatelyn said warmly, patting an upturned barrel beside her. "What would you like to know?"

"Well, the silver dragons protected us during the war. I guess I don't understand how you can call all dragons evil," the girl said, sitting on the barrel and drawing her knees up to her chest.

That was a comment Tatelyn heard often. "What's your name?" she asked.

"Karle."

"Well, Karle, do you know where the first dragons came from?" Karle shook her head. "Reorx forged them from iron, copper, nickel, lead, and tin. Paladine and Takhisis gave them life. But the dragons were rebellious and Takhisis turned them against Paladine. The metals became tarnished, the nickel turning green, the iron red with rust, the copper blue, the lead black, the tin brittle white. Thus the chromatic dragons were born and have served Takhisis ever since."

"I didn't know that," said Karle. "I thought they were always those colors."

Tatelyn nodded and continued her story. "Paladine

missed his children and had Reorx forge them anew, this time from gold, silver, bronze, brass, and copper. The copper had been the most reluctant to turn against Paladine, so he gave it a second chance. Not that they deserved it." Tatelyn could not keep the bitterness from her voice. "So far, they haven't turned against Paladine."

"But they might," Karle said. "Is that what you believe?"

"Anything is possible," Tatelyn said. "Even if they don't turn, they can be possessed. That's what happened to the copper dragon that killed my brother." Tatelyn closed her eyes, willing the tears to stay back. They did, this time.

"They could," Karle agreed. "But I don't think they should be banished from Krynn for something that may not happen."

Before Tatelyn could open her mouth to argue, the girl was gone, flitting down the streets like a spirit. She ducked down an alley and vanished from sight.

Elrit walked over to Tatelyn. "You took a big risk, telling her that. She won't come with us?" He walked with Tatelyn as she approached a little boy on a dirty blanket whose leg had a festering sore.

"No. But it doesn't matter," she said as she laid one hand on the wound and held her medallion of faith with the other. "We aren't going to get anyone here who agrees with us." Tatelyn shook her head, wishing she knew how to convince these people. "The metallic dragons are just as dangerous as the chromatic ones! Without the metallic dragons, we wouldn't have to worry about draconians!"

Elrit said nothing, but nodded, not meeting Tatelyn's eyes. Tatelyn never knew the details of why Elrit followed the Heirs of Huma, but she knew that his parents had been killed and somehow, both a silver dragon and draconians had been involved. Tatelyn had never seen a draconian, but she feared them deeply. She'd even had nightmares of being attacked by the monsters that would have grown up to be dragons had their essences not been twisted out of good dragons' eggs.

"Things were just better before the dragons returned," Tatelyn said, looking up past the dingy walls to the blue sky. The little boy thanked Tatelyn and ran off, yelling something about finding his mother. "Why does no one understand that?"

"Strange words you speak, child," came the raspy voice of an old man who Tatelyn was sure hadn't been standing right next to her a moment ago. He was cleaner than most they had seen there, and as soon as Tatelyn saw his white robes, she knew why. He was a cleric, probably from the temple. Was he here to help the residents of the alley, or rebuke Tatelyn and her friends for combining recruiting with healing?

"Do you know who else returned at the same time as the dragons, who was also viewed with suspicion?" the man asked, coming closer. He reached out toward Tatelyn's throat. Elrit tensed, but she shook her head very slightly and Elrit backed off. The man touched the figure-eight-shaped medallion of Mishakal that Tatelyn wore.

"Mishakal," the old man said, answering his own question. "Many people did not believe she and her consort Paladine meant good tidings for the people of Krynn." The man sat down on a discarded fruit crate across from Tatelyn, folding his legs under him. He seemed rather limber for one so aged.

"It was good fortune that people learned to trust them again so quickly," Tatelyn said.

The man laughed. "My dear, you should have seen the skepticism the early clerics endured: fear, anger, accusations of witchcraft. Had the war not caused so much desperation, we would have faced an even longer battle to be accepted."

"But now we are accepted," Tatelyn said, glancing back toward the temple. "As a healer, I seek to banish what evil I can from this land."

"Yes, I heard your speech. You speak remarkably well for one so young."

Tatelyn blushed at the compliment, though she felt undeserving of it. "I didn't convince anyone today. But I had to try. It's the only way to honor my brother and the plan that Mishakal has for me."

"The plan?" the cleric said. Tatelyn bit her tongue. Few clerics believed her when she spoke of the message she had received, unless they, too, had been harmed by the metallic dragons. However, seeing only open curiosity and concern in the old man's eyes, she decided to tell him.

"A year ago, I entered this temple to become an acolyte. There was a great lady who spoke at our initiation—Lady Crysania."

The old man nodded. "I know her well."

"Do you?" Perhaps this man would be more inclined to believe her mission after all. "I had hoped to speak with her during this visit, but I was told she was gone on a mission. No one would tell me the details or where she went."

"It is a mission she believes to be of utmost importance. Much like your own."

Tatelyn lost all reservations about the cleric. "I wished very much to speak with her. At the acolyte ceremony, she gave a speech about eradicating evil from the land. I wanted to be more than a healer. In the temple, I prayed to Mishakal to give me a mission. As I stood in line with the other acolytes, a brightly colored sunbeam caught my eye. It came from a stained-glass window depicting Huma battling Takhisis."

"I know that window," the cleric said. "It was donated to the church by an old Solamnic family."

Tatelyn barely heard the man, so engrossed was she in her own story. "As I looked at the window, I was overcome with a strong feeling that surely came from Mishakal herself. My mission as a cleric of Mishakal is to rid the world of dragons so that the tragedy that befell my brother and thousands of others will never happen again. Thus, the Heirs of Huma was born."

"A very powerful story," the cleric said. "I am not surprised that you attract so many followers."

None of them citizens of Palanthas, Tatelyn silently noted.

"Would you join us?" Tatelyn asked, surprising herself. She had never worded the question that baldly to anyone.

The man smiled and shook his head. "As you have your mission, I have mine. My place is here, with this church." He looked toward the temple, then back to the alley. "And here, with these people."

Tatelyn didn't feel rebuffed. This man had his own calling, as she had hers. The two stood.

"May I presume to give you a piece of advice, young lady?" the cleric asked.

"Of course," Tatelyn said.

"Don't let the grief for your brother become anger."

The man looked around the alley. It was still crowded, but no one, not even Elrit, was watching them.

"The family that donated that window also gave us this. I think you should have it." The cleric reached into a deep pouch and drew out a small object. He placed it in Tatelyn's palm. It was a broken piece of tarnished jewelry that looked as though it had once been star shaped, but half of the jewel had broken away. Although the silver setting was black with age, the gems studding it glittered like fire in the setting sun.

"I can't accept this!" Tatelyn gasped. "Please, sell it and use it for the church."

The cleric smiled and shook his head. "We couldn't sell something like this. Legend has it that Huma himself once possessed this gem. I can think of no better person to possess it now. Keep it, and may you always be led by the same forces that led Huma." The cleric closed Tatelyn's fingers over the jeweled object.

"I must go. I have much to attend to this evening. I suggest that you and your friends leave the city swiftly, before you're found." He walked in the direction of the temple.

"Wait!" Tatelyn said, running after the man. "You know so much about me, and I don't even know your name."

"You may have heard of me," the cleric said, pushing a jutting stone in the temple wall and revealing a hidden passage back into the temple. "My name is Elistan."

The head of the Church of Paladine winked at her, then ducked into the temple grounds, closing the door behind him before Tatelyn could close her gaping mouth.

CHAPTER TWO

Simle flew straight up into the sky, pointing her nose at the sun. With one last powerful thrust of her wings, she turned about in midair and faced the sapphire Solamnic waters beneath her. Folding her wings behind her and tucking her body to resemble an arrow, she dived straight down into the bay. Her momentum carried her to the bottom, several adult-dragon lengths deep. She touched one claw to the bottom and did a few twirls. So engrossed was she in her acrobatics that she nearly inhaled a passing school of fish when someone tugged her tail.

Behind her, Uncle Nuvar grinned, revealing algae stuck between his large, sharp teeth. He motioned for her to follow him toward the lair. Swimming single file, they approached a narrow opening in the rock at the base of an underwater cliff. Uncle Nuvar lifted the thick strands of seaweed covering the opening and Simle swam past, starting their old game of chase to the treasure hoard through the lair's many winding chambers.

While Simle disliked being in this new land immensely—the lengthy cold season was just one of her many complaints to her parents—she had been happy when her parents announced a few years ago that they were leaving the Dragon Isles. There were too many memories in their old cave. Everywhere Simle looked was a rock like the one that had distracted her while humans stole her siblings. There were many rocks here, of course, but the cave was different and the rocks triggered no sad recollections.

"Have Mother and Father returned yet?" Simle asked her uncle.

"No, but they should soon. They were protecting a group of humans on a pilgrimage. Dangerous land, even now that the war is over."

"Protecting humans?" Simle asked, twisting her mouth. She didn't feel like playing anymore. The thought of humans made Simle's blood boil.

Uncle Nuvar flicked his tongue at her in disapproval. "Little one, you must learn that not all humans are like the ones who stole your siblings. You're old enough now not to see everything in diamond and coal."

"Even if they're not evil, why should we help them? Let them live or die as they choose."

"That's not our way. Before we were sent away from these lands, the bronze dragons were always on good terms with humans." Uncle Nuvar muttered a few low words.

There was a bronze and green flash and the huge dragon disappeared. In his place stood a grown human male who came up to about Simle's wing joint. He had shiny brown hair and a mustache, and wore a rich green cloak trimmed with bronze-colored thread. Only his eyes remained the same, and they twinkled at Simle.

"You know I hate it when you do that." Simle turned to the wall.

"Come now," Uncle Nuvar said, his voice oddly thin and high. "You need to do this yourself. Most Bronzes can change by the time they reach fifty!"

"I can be a bird, or a sunfish, or a crab, or a deer. I can be anything I please, even maybe a kender. But I will *not* take a human form if I live to be fifty thousand!" Simle shrieked, causing a few rocks to tumble from the ceiling. Uncle Nuvar changed back to dragon form. A stalactite that would have impaled his human form bounced harmlessly off his back. He turned Simle around to face him so swiftly that her tail cracked like a whip.

"You must let go of this hatred. Not all humans are evil."

"No, some of them are so weak they need our protection," Simle retorted. "Why should we bother?"

"Because it's right. It's what Paladine wants us to do. Humans do have some redeeming qualities. For one, they can make these amazing gems." Uncle Nuvar bent to pick up something from the pile of treasure, but stopped and listened in the direction of the cave entrance. Far-off splashing echoed through the chamber.

"Mother! Father!" Simle exclaimed, leaping toward the entrance. As soon as her father's head appeared, Simle began to pounce on him, as she did every time he returned from a journey. This time, though, her father's face was not joyous, but filled with dread. Simle altered her jump and landed beside him, suddenly seeing what made her father look so grave.

Simle's father pulled her mother into the cave and laid her on the floor. "Nuvar," he roared. "Go fetch the healer. Fly swiftly!" Uncle Nuvar took one look at the green blood seeping onto the sand and dived through the cave entrance.

"Simle, freshen her bed," Simle's father commanded as he clamped his teeth gently around his mate's neck and dragged her across the floor.

"What's wrong with Mother?" Simle whispered.

"Simle! Do as I say!" Never had Simle's father spoken to her in such a tone. Simle raced to her parents' bed and fluffed the dry seaweed bedding, then added more from the drying rack. Her father laid her mother gently on it. Quickly the seaweed became matted with blood. Simle's father held together the worst wound with his claws as gently as he could. His burning bronze gaze darted to another wound that was almost as bad, then looked at

Simle. Shaking, she stepped forward and pressed the scaled flesh together. She winced as the blood seeped out despite her best attempts to stanch it.

"She's bleeding so much," Simle whispered. "What happened?"

"The pilgrimage was attacked by a band of black dragons." Simle's father used one wing tip to touch Mother's face. "Your mother fought bravely to protect the humans and succeeded, but it was too much for her."

A wave of anger eclipsed Simle's concern for her mother. "Humans again," she spat, releasing a small bit of lightning from her mouth. It struck the sand harmlessly, but her father glared at her.

"There's no time for that now. We would come to their aid again and again if we thought we could prevent one innocent person from being killed."

"And what of my innocent mother?" Simle exclaimed. "If you didn't always help humans you wouldn't be put in danger!"

"Enough!" her father barked, sending a much larger bolt of lightning crackling across the cave. "Your hatred does your mother no good."

More splashing and clattering echoed into their chamber. Simle's father closed his eyes, sighing. "The healer. At last."

Uncle Nuvar escorted the dragon healer, an aged female

Bronze, to Simle's mother's side. She took long strands of kelp and began to bind the wound Simle held together. When the blood ceased trickling through, she turned to Simle.

"Let go, little one," the healer said. "You've done well. Now you serve your mother best by letting me work." Simle nodded and reluctantly moved aside.

Uncle Nuvar took her to the main floor of the cave. They said nothing, but stood and waited for what seemed an eternity. Simle's thoughts flipped back and forth as swiftly as the waves. One moment she was consumed with worry for her mother, the next she burned with hatred for the humans who had, once more, brought pain upon her family.

Finally, the healer and Simle's father moved away from her mother. Uncle Nuvar asked, "How is my sister?"

"She should live," the healer said. "However, she must rest. With wounds such as these, she may never swim or fly again."

Lightning crackled in Simle's throat and she barely managed to swallow it. Never swim or fly? That was almost as dire a pronouncement as death to a bronze dragon. Simle and her family spent much of their time swimming in the ocean, diving, hunting sharks, and searching for pearls. Simle especially liked the times when she and her mother would play swim-and-go-find. And there was nothing as wonderful as flying high above the waves.

Simle looked back toward her mother and saw her blinking heavily. They focused briefly on Simle and a smile twitched the edges of her mouth.

"May I talk to her?" Simle asked.

"Only for a moment," the healer said. "Then she must rest."

Simle walked toward her mother, wanting to run to her side, yet fearful that her footsteps might cause her mother pain. When she reached the nest, she folded her legs under her and knelt before her mother. They touched noses briefly.

"Hello, little one." Her mother's voice was very soft and weak and somewhat slurred, but it was still her mother. "I saved the humans. And they thanked me." Simle's mother then opened her mouth wide and unfurled her long tongue. Wound about the very tip was a long chain. From the chain dangled a very small, very old piece of jewelry.

"Take it," Simle's mother said. At any other time, the effect the object had on her speech would have been comical. Now it only made Simle want to shoot lightning, preferably at humans.

"What is it?" Simle asked, taking the jewel in her claws. It was broken and the silver setting was deeply tarnished, but the glittering gems reminded Simle of the false diamond that distracted her so many years ago.

"Valuable," her mother mumbled. "Wear it. Never

take it off." She watched as Simle wiggled her neck through the chain. The jewel rested between the tops of Simle's front legs.

Her mother nodded and smiled, then her eyes winked shut and her head fell to the side. Simle gasped.

"Father!" she shouted. He raced over to her, looked closely at his mate, then turned to Simle.

"She should be all right. She needs rest, though."

"Will she be able to swim?" Simle asked.

"Only time will tell. Until then, all we can do is wait." Simle's father curled up beside his mate.

Uncle Nuvar came over to Simle then. "Why don't we go for a swim and catch a meal?" Simle gazed at her mother, then nodded and followed Uncle Nuvar back into the ocean.

As they swam, anger began to displace Simle's worry for her mother. How could her mother risk her safety while fighting to help humans? Hadn't humans done enough to her family? Simle had not thought it possible to hate humans more than she had when she woke up that morning, but now her vision was tinged with green rage.

"Uncle Nuvar, where were the humans my parents were protecting?" Simle asked as they swam to deeper waters. She looked about the ocean as though she were searching for sharks, hoping to make her question seem casual.

"They had just reached the Vingaard Mountains when they were attacked. Somewhere to the south." Uncle Nuvar then jerked his head toward a distant shadow. "Sharks!" He swam swiftly toward them, not looking to see if Simle followed.

Simle looked at Uncle Nuvar's slowly fading shadow, then back in the direction of her cave. "I'm sorry, Mother," she said in a whisper. "But I won't stay here and watch you recover or . . . or not. Not while the humans who caused all this are still out there." Simle pointed her nose south and swam along the coast, the jewel thumping against her breast with each stroke.

CHAPTER THREE

A scream awoke Tatelyn. She sat up with a jerk. Where was she? When the dream stupor faded a little she realized she was the one who had screamed.

"Tatelyn? What's wrong?" Ramma's low, soothing voice helped Tatelyn focus and remember where she was. She'd been lying on the floor of the wagon—more a little boxlike house on wheels. They'd been traveling in this wagon for the past week, headed for Tatelyn's hometown, Forestedge. Tatelyn and Ramma sat on a pallet of soft furs and pillows. Ramma's hair gleamed like gold even in the dim sunlight that streamed through the wagon window.

"How much farther?" Tatelyn asked, blinking heavily as the wagon lurched over another rock and thudded back on the ground.

Ramma winced. "Not sure, but for me, I don't think we can get to this town of yours fast enough. And after we convince enough people there to approach the Whitestone

Council, no more traveling for me. I am so very tired of living without luxuries."

Tatelyn stifled a laugh as she looked around the wagon she and Ramma shared. It was a good thing that clerics like herself didn't accumulate many possessions, because there was barely room for Tatelyn's few belongings amid Ramma's spellbooks, magical artifacts, and numerous outfits. Tatelyn never knew that there were so many shades of white until she saw Ramma's wardrobe.

Bored, Tatelyn took out the jewel that Elistan had given to her and examined it yet again. In the wagon's dim light it looked utterly unremarkable. The metal was so tarnished it resembled wrought iron, and none of the jewels sparkled at all.

"Still no idea why Elistan gave that to you?" Ramma asked, leaning over Tatelyn's shoulder to peer at it. "Looks like it spent the last hundred years under the sea."

"No idea at all." Tatelyn gave the jewel one last look, then tucked it back in her pouch. "I wish he hadn't been so cryptic."

"I've been scouring my books but still haven't found anything on it," Ramma said, picking up another book and flipping through it. "I just can't shake the feeling that I've seen it before."

"I don't know where you could have, but keep looking," Tatelyn said. "It must have some importance, and for Revered Son Elistan to give me something like this puzzles me."

Ramma nodded, settled back on a cushion, and began reading.

At midday they stopped for a meal, setting up a small cookfire and roasting a brace of rabbits Elrit had caught during the morning journey. Elrit's family, part wild Kagonesti elves and part Ergothian sailors, had often had to live off the land, and his hunting skills served the journey well. The entire group now numbered about twenty people, all of them from humble backgrounds like Tatelyn and Elrit, with the exception of Ramma, Rogan, and a couple of Rogan's friends. Their food supplies had to stretch further now than they'd needed on the journey to Palanthas.

Despite worries about the food supply, Tatelyn couldn't help but obsess over recruitment. As she chewed a piece of stale jerky, she hoped they could get enough followers in Forestedge.

As if reading her thoughts, Elrit said, "Perhaps we could go to my mother's homeland after this. The Kagonesti may be willing to support the Heirs of Huma."

"But why would the elves help us?" Ramma asked. "We're mostly a human group, after all."

Tatelyn glared at her. "We have to try. This is far too important."

"Indeed," Rogan said, sitting down on a tree stump. His bulky armor made it too difficult to sit on the ground. "I think I may return to Palanthas after we visit Forestedge."

"Return?" Elrit scoffed. "They'll have your head on a pike!"

"Not if I do it right," Rogan said. "If I approach each knight alone, not in public, I could show them what the dragons have done to the knighthood: thrown it into disarray, put people of lesser bloodlines in power. . . ." Rogan shook his head. "If my father were alive he'd've helped us. He spoke out against trusting the silver dragons when they first returned. Because of them, our uncle Derek and our father and so many others lost their power in the knighthood."

Elrit and Tatelyn exchanged glances. Although Rogan and Ramma had proved valuable in gaining the support of some nobles, Rogan often went off like this, raving about the destruction of the knighthood. Tatelyn's only tactic up to this point had been to just nod and change the subject as soon as possible, but it was getting worse and she was starting to worry.

"We should move out," Elrit said. "We can reach the village in an hour or two if we keep up the pace."

Tatelyn didn't return to the wagon with Ramma, but instead walked with Elrit on the ever-steeper road.

It was easier to climb over and around the rocks than to be jostled by riding over them in the wagon.

She also wanted to see her village the moment it was within sight. It was still bright midafternoon when she saw Forestedge for the first time in a year.

When Tatelyn left home, they had just begun to rebuild from the sorceress Asvoria's destruction. It now looked like the villagers had rebuilt most of the major buildings, such as the store and the blacksmith's forge, in the same locations. They had reconstructed many of the houses as well, but so few compared to the number that filled the village before the dragon came. Looking around, Tatelyn could see why. Despite the village's seeming recovery, so many familiar faces were gone forever—including her brother Brigg's.

The last thing Tatelyn had seen before her world changed forever was a copper dragon. Immediately after she and her brother spotted it blotting out the sun, the ground beneath them erupted and Brigg was slain by a giant zombie worm controlled by that copper dragon. Tatelyn had escaped and raised the alarm at the village. The warning was too late for Brigg, though.

Elrit laid a hand on Tatelyn's shoulder. "Will you be all right?"

Tatelyn nodded, blinking quickly so the others would not see her tears. Her village was returning to normal. She should be thankful for that. She shouldn't dwell in the past. Everywhere she looked, people were hard at work rebuilding. And her parents still lived. Elrit had no home and no parents—both were now at the bottom of the Blood Sea.

"You go visit first, Tatelyn," Elrit said. "The rest of us will set up camp here." Already Rogan was settling the wagon in a secure spot under a cluster of trees while Ramma used her magic to light a fire. Tatelyn flashed a quick smile at Elrit, then walked up the dirt path toward home.

Before the dragon, Tatelyn's family had lived on the outskirts of the village. Her father liked being close to the forest, and Tatelyn and Brigg had spent most of their childhood running through the trees. But after their home was destroyed, Tatelyn's parents decided to rebuild closer to the village center. More people and fewer trees around their home meant fewer reminders of Brigg. It didn't matter to Tatelyn, though. If her parents had rebuilt in the middle of Palanthas, visiting them would still bring memories of Brigg flooding over her.

"Tatelyn? Is that you?" A tall girl who looked to be just shy of twenty called to Tatelyn from a vegetable garden. She walked to the garden fence, then dropped her basket of carrots and raced toward Tatelyn. Her long, blonde braid flew out behind her as she ran.

"Marin!" Tatelyn squealed as she and the other girl collided in an embrace. Marin had been Brigg's closest friend his entire life. Tatelyn used to tease Brigg about being sweet on Marin, but he never gave her a straight answer.

"You're a cleric!" Marin said, gazing at the blue robes and medallion. "Your parents told us where you went and read parts of your letters home, but to see you . . ." Marin looked down at her dirt-streaked skirt and sighed. "I've never left Forestedge. You've done so much and it's only been a year!"

"I've done much more than become a cleric," Tatelyn said. "I won't say much now, but I have something in mind that everyone in Forestedge can do. Something that can help us recover from Asvoria's attack."

A swift shadow of pain fell over Marin's face. "We *are* recovering, Tatelyn," she said. "The dead were buried long ago. We're rebuilding."

"I have something much more in mind," Tatelyn said. Marin tilted her head and raised an eyebrow. Tatelyn wanted to tell her more, but then remembered her parents. "I must go and see Mother and Father. But I'll see you again before I leave."

"Of course," said Marin as she turned back to the garden. "Go spend time with your folks. We'll speak later." Marin went back to picking carrots and did not look at Tatelyn as she journeyed down the road.

Tatelyn wondered at Marin's reaction. Didn't she want to do something to avenge Brigg's death, her own father's death? But thoughts of Marin disappeared as she saw her parents' new home. When she left, they had only built the wooden frame. Now, there was a small, neat cottage set among a cluster of other similar houses. As Tatelyn neared the door, she paused. She missed them, but what would seeing them do to her?

A cluster of oak leaves was pinned to the door. Oaks had been Brigg's favorite tree. Tatelyn raised one hand, hesitated, then knocked just beneath the oak leaves.

The door opened and a woman with dark hair and violet eyes the same shade as Tatelyn's stepped out. The violet eyes widened, then crinkled with the rest of the woman's face into a smile.

"Tatelyn!" she exclaimed. Tatelyn pushed aside the memories of Brigg, only for a moment, and stepped into her mother's arms as though she were a young child once more.

Tatelyn's father, having received the news that a strange girl cloaked in blue had entered his house, had dropped his hammer midstroke and run all the way from the new market area straight into Tatelyn's arms. Tatelyn returned his embrace, but the sight of her father shocked her. He had simultaneously aged and grown to resemble Brigg. Not Brigg as he lived, though, but the sight of Brigg as he lay upon the ground dead, the sight that still haunted Tatelyn's dreams. Her father looked like Brigg had at that moment, the life sapped out of him. The change made it difficult for Tatelyn to meet his eyes, however bad she felt about not returning his gaze.

"We received your letter about the Heirs of Huma. Tell us more." Her mother spooned more venison and potatoes onto Tatelyn's wooden plate, a midafternoon meal that her mother had whipped up when she heard how long it had been since Tatelyn had eaten a home-cooked meal. Tatelyn chewed slowly before responding.

"We have about fifty people in various towns and villages across Solamnia. We organize groups of five or seven in each settlement, then move on to the next. It allows the movement to keep growing."

"You'll find many more here in Forestedge." Tatelyn's father drained his mug of ale. "No one has forgotten what that copper dragon did to us. We're still rebuilding."

Tatelyn's mother nodded. "If you like, we could have a town meeting arranged by nightfall. We told them what you're doing. Everyone's glad that someone is finally addressing what a menace the metallic dragons are."

"Not everyone," Tatelyn's father cautioned. "But most.

Your mother and I especially. I worried when you decided to join the clerics of these new gods, but it appears that the path you chose is a good one."

Tatelyn's heart warmed to hear her parents say this. Although they had not tried to stop her from seeking out the clerics of Mishakal, they had been suspicious of the new gods and their followers, as had many people. When the gods returned to the world after so many centuries gone, people couldn't help but wonder what it meant, for good or ill. That her parents trusted her and would help her made Tatelyn's confidence grow.

"That's a wonderful idea," Tatelyn said. "My friends and I had hoped to talk with people individually, but a town meeting would be a perfect forum."

Tatelyn's father stood up from the table. "I'll spread the word. Come to the market at moonrise with your friends."

"Thank you so much, Father." Tatelyn rose as well. "I hate to leave now, Mother, but . . ."

Tatelyn's mother made a flapping motion with her hands. "Go on, girl, this is more important. If what you do prevents even one more person from death at the claws of those vicious beasts, go forth and do what you must."

Tatelyn hugged both her parents, then ran back to where the others set up camp. She began shouting before she could smell the fire Ramma had built.

"They're holding a town meeting for us!" she said as she skidded to a halt before running into Elrit. "We might be able to do all our work in one night!"

Ramma looked up from mending a tear in an ivory robe. "We'd best prepare, then," she said. "This could be our most important meeting ever."

"More important than Palanthas?" Rogan asked, sounding a bit perturbed. "Ramma and I recruited knights and important families there."

"We have money from the families of Palanthas, and force from the knights," Tatelyn agreed. "But look at this town." She waved in the direction of the newly built structures and freshly plowed fields, between which could still be seen numerous areas of scorched earth. "There's not a family in this town who didn't lose a loved one in Asvoria's attack. This is where we find passion," Tatelyn said.

As the moons rose in the dark sky above the forested Vingaard Mountains, the four companions walked into town. Tatelyn wondered what they thought of her home village. It probably looked crude and poor to Ramma and Rogan. One never knew what Elrit thought about such things.

"Oh my," Ramma said, slowing. For a moment Tatelyn thought the wizard was going to make a comment about the condition of the town. Then she saw what Ramma was looking at. In the center of town was a glowing circle of lanterns. As more people approached, the lanterns multiplied and moved toward the center of the circle.

"Are they all here for us?" Ramma whispered. "I had no idea there were so many people in Forestedge."

"There aren't," Tatelyn said, puzzled. "Not even before the attack." Tatelyn recognized only about one in every three people. "Where did they come from?"

"From other villages that fell prey to Asvoria after she possessed the copper dragon."

Tatelyn turned to see her father, who was beaming almost as brightly as the light that shone from his lantern. "When I told the workers at the market, a few of the younger men found the fastest horses in town and rode to spread the word."

"This is far more than I ever dreamed!" Tatelyn said. "Thank you!"

"No, our thanks to you, Tatelyn," a voice behind her said. Tatelyn recognized Horao, Marin's uncle. "You started something that could change the fate of Krynn forever."

Tatelyn could not respond and did not have time to even if she could speak. Tatelyn's mother and father pushed her toward the podium at the center of the market square. She looked to Ramma.

"Should we all speak?" Tatelyn asked. Whenever they

spoke to a group, they all took turns telling their personal stories. Palanthas was the first place they'd been unable to do so, but that was hardly their fault.

Ramma shook her head. "Not tonight. These people don't want to hear our stories. They want to hear someone who knows how they suffered."

Tatelyn nodded and walked up the wooden steps to the podium. She looked up at the figure-eight constellation of Mishakal. Whispering a prayer for strength, she turned to face the crowd.

Tatelyn had spoken of Brigg's death many times in front of many people. Never before, however, had she spoken to people who knew him, who had lost so many of their own family and friends in the same manner. Tears filled her eyes and her throat closed. The only thing that kept her talking was the sight of her parents in the first row.

"When I first saw the copper dragon, I felt only awe. It was so beautiful. I had always heard that the metallic dragons meant us no harm, so I stood and looked at it. I called Brigg to ask if he could see it. While we were distracted by it, the zombie worm rose from the ground and Brigg . . ."

She could not tell of Brigg's death, but for once, she didn't have to. She heard faint sobs from the crowd. Tatelyn gulped and said, "We know now that dragon was possessed by an evil sorceress. It was once good, but it was still dangerous. If the dragons are banished from Krynn, as they were before, we could remove that danger. We exist only at the whim of these creatures. The good dragons could turn on us at any moment, by magic, by coercion, by their own choice. And what of draconians? They come from the eggs of good dragons. If those eggs were no longer around, no more draconians could be created."

Tatelyn expected the scoffs to begin now, as they did at so many places. But here, people nodded and murmured sounds of agreement.

"I propose that at the next Whitestone Council, we approach them and speak our piece about the so-called good dragons. We persuade those in power to convince the dragons to leave Solamnia."

Now crickets were the only sound Tatelyn heard. They don't want to hear me, Tatelyn thought with sudden certainty. They wish I had never come back to dredge up their memories.

Then one lone person began clapping. The clapping grew louder and less scattered until it sounded like a heartbeat pounding from the earth itself. Tatelyn's parents smiled at her, their own hands coming together with the rest of the villagers'.

"Stop!" a voice shrieked. The thudding applause stopped immediately and everyone turned to look to the back, where Marin stood on a bench and addressed the crowd.

"We all suffered at the hands of Asvoria. She destroyed so much of what we hold dear here. But the copper dragon was possessed!" she yelled, her face pale. "It never would've attacked us otherwise. The good dragons returned to save us and they did! And this is how we repay them?"

"If the copper dragon wasn't around to possess, how far would that sorceress have gotten?" Tatelyn's mother shouted back at Marin. The audience rippled with agreement. "If the dragons leave, they can't be used for evil purposes!"

The crowd grew so loud that Marin stepped down off the bench. She looked at Tatelyn once, and the sorrow in her eyes was so great that Tatelyn couldn't hold her gaze. Marin slipped out of the crowd among hisses as folk crowded the podium, seeking to join the Heirs of Huma.

CHAPTER FOUR

Simle could barely see the ground passing beneath her for her tears. She left home two days ago and had never been so miserable. Always before when times were bad, even during that horrible day when her siblings were stolen, her parents had been there. Her mother always had a joke or some funny expression to make Simle and her father laugh until they all had small lightning bolts flashing across the cave. Simle's father always managed to find the bright side or, if there really was no bright side, at least some small hope. In the darkest days, they comforted her with just their presence. Without them, Simle found herself unable to laugh, sinking more into despair with every passing moment. What if her mother died?

Diving slowly to the ground, Simle shuddered. She needed to rest. Never before had she flown so far, and her wings hurt dreadfully. She had kept to the water during the first part of her journey, but she soon found that the seas close to land were monitored by the good dragons, and she didn't want them asking what a youngling like her was doing alone. She needed to go inland anyway if she was to find the humans responsible for her mother's injuries.

Simle landed on the bank of a river near the foot of a mountain. Being so far from the ocean made her nervous. At least there was water here. She dipped her head into it and took a long sip, then immediately spit the water back out. Coughing, she glared at the river. What kind of water was that? There wasn't the least bit of salt in it, and it was filthy!

Filthy or not, it appeared to be the only large water source she was likely to find in this part of the land. Simle waded into the river, which only came to her neck at its deepest point. There were, however, many small fish swimming around. Simle settled on the bottom of the river, holding very still, and waited for a fish to swim close to her. When one ventured near, she stretched her neck and snapped her jaws around it. She caught ten fish this way, but they were so small she still felt hungry. Her poor stomach would never fill up at this rate—the biggest fish she could see was a speck compared to her normal shark dinners. There weren't any pearls either. Simle really wanted a pearl right now.

What did humans eat? Simle wondered. She knew humans sometimes raised animals for food rather than hunting. They had to keep those animals somewhere.

Perhaps she could find a human settlement and steal them. Simle rose out of the river and shook off the grimy water, frowning at the residue it left on her shiny bronze scales.

She decided to walk rather than fly. Her wings were sore from so much use. Soon after she started off, she saw smoke rising above the trees. She'd seen fires like this earlier as she flew from the sea. She'd first thought it meant the forest was on fire, but soon she learned the truth: There were humans nearby.

Any humans close by couldn't help but hear Simle's steps crunching over the underbrush. Still, she tried to step as lightly as possible. After snapping a very loud branch, however, Simle sighed. This was ridiculous. She could fly over the village and take them by surprise.

Before she took off, however, she wanted to practice her lightning strikes in case the humans attacked her. Simle had never used them intentionally to harm any-thing—her parents forbade that—but she loosed them all the time by accident. How hard could it be? Simle took a deep breath, flexed the muscles in her throat, and aimed at a fallen tree free enough from dry brush that she wouldn't set the forest on fire.

Nothing happened. Simle tried again, but she couldn't emit the tiniest spark, let alone a well-formed bolt of lightning. She coughed, slapped the back of her claws against her throat, and tried once more. Nothing.

Simle was strongly reminded of the time she got hiccups after eating half a shark too fast. She hadn't liked the hiccups, but once they were finally gone she'd wanted to feel them again. She tried to hiccup to bring the lightning, but could not.

Simle sighed. Perhaps she wasn't old enough to control it. It hadn't occurred to her that she couldn't do it yet. She thought it was only because she had never really tried. She attempted it once more and succeeded only in straining a muscle deep in her throat. Her tail quivered in frustration.

Well, she would simply have to make do with what she had. Simle took another deep breath and called on different muscles in her neck. A small cloud emerged from her mouth, dissipating into the air. Simle was immune to its effects, but she could tell that this breath weapon was working, and working well. Another test puff, and Simle spread her wings and took to the air.

Following the smoke, Simle found the village quickly. On a small rise overlooking the village, several humans had set up an encampment. Some wore shiny metal that must have been armor, some wore the blue robes of the goddess Mishakal, and one was dressed in the white robes of a wizard. One of the armored humans looked up and yelled loudly, drawing the others' attention to Simle, then sent a long, sharp stick at Simle. She ducked, but then a blast of magic caught Simle on her underbelly. The humans were attacking her!

Mother and Father lied, they lied! The thought screamed in Simle's mind as she flew higher and turned around for an attack of her own. They lied! As Simle dived toward the ground she recognized the metal armor as that belonging to a Knight of Solamnia. White-robed wizards, clerics of Mishakal—these were all people that her parents told her were the allies of the good dragons. Yet they were attacking her! Well, Simle had a few surprises of her own. She was young, but she was hardly helpless.

Simle pulled into a steep dive. As the figures on the ground grew nearer, she inhaled deeply. When she was only a great wyrm's length from the ground, she pulled out of her dive and released her breath upon the figures. They began coughing and hacking and holding their hands over their pitifully small noses. They weren't sending any more attacks her way, at least for now. Simle smiled and flew toward the forest at the foot of the mountain. She could rest there, then continue on to find the humans responsible for her mother's injuries.

At the very edge of the forest was a small farm. Nothing grew here, but the house and land looked like other farms that Simle had passed during her journey—except this house was destroyed and no people tilled the fallow fields. It looked like the forest and wild grass were overtaking this land. As it should be, Simle thought, growing angry. Humans did nothing but manipulate the earth to suit their own ends, putting up those "buildings" all over it. Why didn't they all live in caves, like the dwarves?

Movement on the ground caught Simle's eye. The farm was not abandoned completely. A human with black hair twined in numerous braids knelt on the ground. She did not look at the sky, but rather the earth in front of her, running her hands through the soil. She wore blue robes—robes that were identical to the clerics with the group that had attacked her. Well, this girl was not going to attack first.

Simle dived down at the human with a roar. The girl looked up at Simle, her deep violet eyes widening. Simle faltered in the air. Something was amiss with this girl. As their gazes locked, Simle was startled by the expression in the girl's eyes—those violet eyes blazed with hatred. Simle landed, not on top of the girl as she had planned, but a short distance away. She could not bring herself to come closer.

Not since she was a tiny wyrmling had Simle been so close to a human. The girl's head only came to about Simle's shoulder, and she was much, much thinner. She looked a bit like the deer Simle had seen running about the forest, except that she walked on two legs—like Uncle Nuvar had the day she left. Her eyes, though, were the eyes of a shark.

Neither girl nor dragon lifted their intense gaze. Simle then noticed the girl was not coughing. Had Simle's other breath weapon failed her as well? No, Simle could smell traces of it in the air. The girl's lips moved and her hand went to a medallion she wore around her neck: two circles linked together.

The girl's eyes frightened Simle to her very core. Did all humans have such hate in their eyes? The girl took a step toward Simle. Startled, Simle took to the sky in one leap. She glanced back at the diminishing figure of the girl, shuddered, then continued toward the forest on the mountainside.

"My mother would not fear that girl," Simle said. A sizzling tear fell and began to eat away at a rock far below.

CHAPTER FIVE

atelyn didn't really have the time to spare from recruiting. Still, she couldn't leave Forestedge until she saw one place—the place where Brigg died.

Years ago, she and her family lived on a farm on the outskirts of town, right next to the forest that spread up the Vingaard Mountains like moss creeping over a rock. Since Tatelyn had left, the huge oak tree that grew next to the house had fallen over, perhaps from a storm, perhaps from rot. It had cleft the remains of the small wooden building in two as neatly as a knife through a roast. Tatelyn paused to look at it only for a moment. It was not the house that she needed to see, but the field behind it.

Brigg and her father had kept the forest at bay by chopping trees and weeding the saplings that were always popping up in the field. Now the forest was beginning to reclaim the field. Instead of walking through freshly plowed earth or shafts of wheat, Tatelyn now had to walk amid young trees. Still, she knew exactly where she had stood that day. She walked to the precise spot where she first saw the copper dragon. She knelt on the ground and ran her hands over the earth. Closing her eyes, she could still hear the roar of the ground opening to release the horrifying worm that the copper dragon controlled.

The last moment I was happy was the moment I saw that copper dragon, Tatelyn thought as she looked up. Then she gasped. For a moment she thought she the past was coming to life.

Right in front of her, a dragon roared as it approached.

This dragon was smaller than the one who killed Brigg, but still it cast a shadow larger than two houses. It was a slightly different color too—more brown than copper, with green edging the wings. She glared at it. How dare it come here? Could she not be in peace from a dragon even in this place, the one place she had avoided for so long?

The dragon landed nearby and flapped its wings briskly. The breeze carried a faint stench to Tatelyn, but she never took her eyes off the dragon. It regarded her with horrible bronze eyes. Tatelyn whispered a prayer to Mishakal to take her fear away and the goddess obliged. The fear vanished from her heart, but was replaced by hate.

Tatelyn and the dragon glared at each other for what seemed an eternity, then, with a flap of wings that blew

Tatelyn's hair and cloak back, the dragon took to the sky and flew toward the forest, away from town. Relief flooded Tatelyn, but then a horrible thought occurred to her. Had the dragon gone to the town first?

Tatelyn raced to the village, where nothing looked amiss. She ran to her parents' home and burst in the door. The two of them were sitting down to a meal and looked up at her in surprise.

"You're all right!" Tatelyn exclaimed.

"Of course we're all right," said her mother, handing her a piece of freshly baked bread. "Why wouldn't we be?"

"There was a dragon," Tatelyn gasped, squeezing the bread in her hands. "Out in the fields. It could have been a copper. I thought it had . . ."

Tatelyn's parents exchanged dark glances. "We didn't see it," her mother answered. "But why did it come here?"

"I don't know." Tears of rage trickled down Tatelyn's cheeks.

"No harm done here," her father said, patting Tatelyn's shoulder.

"That's not the point," Tatelyn snapped. Her parents looked at her, startled. "This is only one more reason why these creatures should be banished. They shouldn't be allowed to just show up and frighten us at their whim. We need to do something."

Tatelyn's mother and father both nodded. "Go,

then," her mother said. "You keep meeting with people who can help banish those vile creatures. You're doing important work."

Tatelyn kissed her parents farewell and hurried back to the encampment. It wasn't far out of town and she wanted to be sure everyone there was well too.

"Tatelyn!" Ramma waved frantically. "Help me with Elrit. He was hit bad."

Elrit lay on the ground, coughing. Tatelyn caught a whiff of the horrific smell and waved a hand in front of her face. It smelled as though someone had set up a slaughterhouse in a privy.

"It wasn't this bad when the dragon landed by me," Tatelyn said as she knelt by Elrit. She whispered a prayer and his breathing eased.

"We attacked it," Rogan said, sticking his sword in the ground. "I would've given anything for a dragonlance. But Elrit got off a few good shots at it."

Ramma glared at him. "I hit it with magic as well."

Rogan continued talking to Tatelyn as though Ramma had not said a word. "It attacked us with its breath. Most of us are all right now, but Elrit got the worst of it. Was anyone hurt in town?"

"It didn't go to town, thank Mishakal," Tatelyn said. "I saw it, though, outside town."

"Did it attack you?" Elrit sat up with a grimace. Everyone

kneeling around him backed away a pace, covering their noses. He still smelled awful.

"No. It smelled bad, but nothing like here. Ramma, do you happen to have any of that fine Palanthian perfume?"

Ramma ducked into the wagon and emerged with a small bottle. She uncorked it and reached as far as she could without touching Elrit, holding it under Elrit's nose.

Rogan snorted. "Where on Krynn did you expect to need that?"

"A lady never travels without perfume," Ramma said, pitching her voice in her best formal-banquet tone. Everyone giggled except Rogan, who stalked off. Ramma rolled her eyes at him and took the perfume back to the wagon.

"What was that about?" Tatelyn whispered to Elrit.

"Sibling skirmish," Elrit said, then clapped a hand over his mouth. "I'm so sorry! You went to see where Brigg . . ."

Tatelyn looked at the tips of her leather shoes peeking from under her robe. "It's all right. Anything you say couldn't hurt me more than the sight of that dragon. I stood in the exact same place I was when Brigg and I first saw the copper dragon. Then the dragon that attacked camp landed in the field in front of me."

"So you saw it too," Elrit said. "Did it breathe on you as well?"

"No. It didn't do anything. *I* didn't do anything." Tatelyn hit the ground next to her. "I stood there in front of a dragon and I couldn't do anything!"

Rogan walked back to them, rubbing his hands together. There was a new light in his blue eyes, a light that made Tatelyn wary.

"Would you like to do something?" Rogan asked Tatelyn. "Something more than recruiting people and convincing them that the metallic dragons are just as dangerous as the chromatic dragons?"

"You know I would, more than anything."

Elrit and Rogan exchanged glances. "I have an idea," Rogan said. "I wasn't sure anyone would want to attempt it. But now . . ."

"What is it?"

Rogan leaned close to Tatelyn. "What about capturing the dragon?"

Surely Rogan was joking. But Rogan rarely jested. In fact Tatelyn couldn't remember a time he'd ever really had a good laugh. Now he looked even more serious than usual.

"We can do it," Rogan said. "Especially with all the people we have now. All we need to do is track the dragon and capture it."

"Oh, that's *all*, is it?" Elrit butted in. "Just how do you propose we might do that?"

"It's small," Rogan said, starting a fire. It was past time for supper, which the dragon's attack had delayed. "Not even an adult. It didn't throw any lightning at us, which probably means it's too young to do so. The only weapon it has is stench, and with the right preparation we can handle that."

"That is *not* its only weapon!" Tatelyn exclaimed. "Are you forgetting the claws? Teeth? The fact that it can fly?" Tatelyn saw her friends' downcast faces and tried to explain. "I do want to do this, I really do. But we can't forget how dangerous these creatures are."

"Tatelyn, your entire town would help us with this," Rogan said. "They can fight, set traps, track the dragon. If we set archers to shoot its wings, it won't be able to fly and we can fight it on the ground."

Tatelyn pictured the scenario in her mind. It could work, but something about this didn't seem right.

"Give me a night to think about it," Tatelyn said finally. "I'll pray to Mishakal about this. We can discuss it further in the morning." She didn't talk to anyone the rest of the evening, silently going through the motions of eating and washing up as she pondered what was holding her back.

Tatelyn's parents had originally offered to open their

home to her and her friends, but even after spending time with them, Tatelyn thought that spending the night under the same roof with them, but not Brigg, would be too much for her. I must be focused, she thought, not sorrowful. Tatelyn spread her bedroll under a canvas awning stretched between the wagon and two trees. She lay there for a while, watching the stars appear over the horizon. How could she sleep? She wasn't the least bit tired and her mind raced with the questions that the day had brought up.

The others fell asleep one by one, except for Rogan. He would watch for dragons the first part of the night, then a villager from Forestedge would relieve him. Tatelyn sighed and put her hand over her eyes to block the firelight.

"Tatelyn?"

How would she ever get to sleep if people kept waking her? Tatelyn sat up and opened her eyes, cranky and ready to grump at someone.

An old woman dressed in a sky blue robe knelt by the fire. She smiled at Tatelyn and held something up to the fire. Glittering rainbows spread across the woman's face as she turned the item over.

"Come here, child," the woman said. Tatelyn rose and walked over. The woman was holding the jewel Elistan had given Tatelyn. Tatelyn reached into her pouch, sure the woman had stolen the jewel from her. But her own jewel was still there. Tatelyn held it in the firelight as well. Light danced between the two jewels as though they spoke to each other.

"This jewel is very beautiful," the woman said. "You should not hide it away." She pulled on her jewel and molten metal stretched out from the points until it transformed into a fine chain. She held out one hand to Tatelyn. Without thinking, Tatelyn put her jewel in the woman's hands. The lady chuckled.

"Wealth does not rule you, my dear. Good." The woman fastened the chain to the jewel and held it up. It spun, catching the fire and reflecting light across the woman's and Tatelyn's faces.

"This belonged to Huma once," the woman said.

Tatelyn nodded as an idea struck her. "Will it help us capture a dragon? Is that what Huma used it for?"

"Huma had his own path to walk. The lessons he learned were his alone. You will have your own path and lessons." The woman contemplated the gem. "Still, I think this might help you."

Tatelyn bowed and the woman slipped the necklace over her head. As she lifted Tatelyn's braids over the necklace, she brushed Tatelyn's neck. In that instant, Tatelyn knew who she was.

"Mishakal." Tatelyn began to kneel, but the woman shook her head and pulled Tatelyn to her feet.

"You needed my advice, so I came." Mishakal smiled at her. "What would you ask of me?"

"Should we try to capture the dragon?" Tatelyn asked without hesitation.

"Your fate and that of the bronze dragon are intertwined." The woman smiled at Tatelyn. "I can tell you no more. I wish you good fortune on your quest." Blue light began to emanate from the woman, growing brighter and brighter. Tatelyn closed her eyes against the brilliance. When she opened them again, she was in her bedroll, the first pale morning light creeping over her.

As Tatelyn sat up, something rolled across her chest. Looking down, she saw the jewel hanging from a fine chain about her neck, next to the medallion of Mishakal. Tatelyn smiled.

The others were already awake and fixing breakfast. They all turned to Tatelyn as she walked toward them. No one said anything, but the question was in their eyes.

"Mishakal came to me in a dream," Tatelyn said, clasping her necklace. "We will capture the dragon."

CHAPTER SIX

Simle spent the night in a cave on the riverbank. The water, though murky and not salty, offered some comfort to her. Still, she couldn't push her mother out of her mind. She ached to return home, but as long as she stayed away, there was a chance that her mother could still be alive. If she came home and found her dead, though . . .

Whimpering, Simle curled tightly into a ball. This cave was not as warm as home. Although her parents were not able to find a volcano as they would have preferred when they left the Dragon Isles, at least the cave was toasty during all but the very coldest months. Simle closed her eyes and fell asleep. She dreamed of home, and bronze eggs hatching, and humans vanishing suddenly from all of Krynn.

Simle awoke to a rumbling in her belly. She had not taken any animals from the town as she had planned. Maybe now was a good time to try some of the creatures she'd seen yesterday in the fields. Some had thick white fur while others were white with black spots. Simle thought the fur looked rather icky, like eating dried seaweed. Perhaps she should try them, in any case. The few plants she'd tried were bitter and did little to assuage her hunger. She would fill her belly, then continue her search for the humans responsible for her mother's injuries. She had no idea what she would do with them once she caught them. Perhaps it might be satisfying to breathe on them and watch them choke so hard they bent double.

Simle emerged from the cave and began to walk back to the village. She thought about flying but decided she would see prey better on the ground, especially in the forest. Walking through the forest was very much like being underwater. The light filtering through the leaves created rippling patterns like waves. The wind moved the branches just like water did. Underwater there were fish; here there were birds. Simle watched as a flock of them flew out from the trees ahead of her. They were pretty to watch. When fish acted like that, something was after them. What was chasing the birds?

Even though Simle thought she could handle anything in this land, she thought that perhaps now was the time to observe, not go barreling into something unknown. Her wounds from yesterday were minor, but they still stung. Simle closed her eyes, muttered *"Perubahan saya,"* and felt a pop and a rushing of air in her ears as though flying at top speed. When she opened her eyes she was much lower to the ground and her injuries no longer pained her. After inspecting the fur and tiny paws of her new squirrel form, she scampered up a tree to observe.

She had polymorphed just in time. She heard rustling nearby that grew louder and louder, and Simle saw a group of humans come out of a tangle of underbrush and stand directly below her. She twitched her tail angrily. It was the humans who had attacked her yesterday. Simle fought the urge to transform back right then and there. The forest was too closed in. She couldn't maneuver well or take to the air. Better to watch and listen.

"That's odd," said a dark-skinned human, bending close to the ground. No, not completely human, Simle realized. The pointed ears and slender build marked him a half-elf. He was the one who had shot arrows at Simle. She stifled a squeak of indignation and bent down to listen better.

"The dragon's tracks end here." The half-elf straightened and looked around the forest. "No more tracks, no more broken branches. It couldn't have flown away through those trees." He pointed up in the direction of Simle, where she sat observing the group in a thick tangle of branches.

"That ridiculous, Elrit," said the armor-clad human. "You must be reading the tracks wrong. How could a dragon just disappear?"

"If you read half as much as you fought, brother," said a white-robed female whom Simle recognized as the wizard from yesterday, "you would know that these creatures can change into others. The dragon is here. It just took another form." The humans looked about the forest and Simle ducked into a hole in the tree. They couldn't find her here, but her little squirrel heart pounded. She would wait until they had moved on, then transform back and leave this horrid place. She had not expected to be hunted in this world of humans.

"That's what makes the dragons so tricky." A new voice joined the three. "They can take any form they wish. You never know where they may be hiding. We must find this one and capture it."

Simle peeked through a crack in the tree and this time could not contain her squeak of surprise. The new voice belonged to the girl who had stared at Simle with such hate. The girl turned toward the tree and Simle froze, forgetting for a moment that a layer of bark hid her from the girl's sight. A glimmer of colored light caught Simle's eye. She looked closer at the girl and nearly lost her grip on the bark. The girl wore the other half of the pendant that Simle's mother had given her!

Simle gave them a high-pitched chitter. She had found the humans responsible for her mother's injuries! How else would the girl have the same necklace?

The humans all looked around, but still couldn't see her. Simle forgot the lack of cover, forgot that she was in a tree, forgot that she was outnumbered. She transformed back into a dragon, sending bark and leaves and limbs everywhere as she exploded from the trunk.

The humans all cried out in surprise, but recovered their wits quickly. The armored human drew his sword and advanced on Simle. She swiped at him with her claws and knocked him into a shrub. His armor had protected him, however, and he was soon back on his feet. The wizard was digging into her pouches with a look of concentration and Simle knew that in moments she would face more arcane weapons. The half-elf had drawn his bow and aimed an arrow at Simle.

She inhaled and exhaled quickly at the humans. They fell back, coughing. Simle tried to call on her lightning breath, but it still was out of her control. Roaring in frustration, she swung her tail in a wide arc, knocking the wizard to the ground.

She had to get the girl with the necklace away from the others. What was so valuable to her that was worth the life of a dragon? Looking around at the trees, Simle calculated her escape. If she could break through the line of humans, she could fly away as soon as she reached a clearing. The girl was small. Surely Simle could take her and get some answers.

An arrow whistled over Simle's back. The half-elf was shooting at her wings! If he hit them, she would never be able to fly. Simle lowered her head, folded her wings tightly, and ran at the girl in blue.

The violet eyes widened in shock as Simle galloped toward her. The girl started to duck out of the way, but Simle was too quick. She ran into the girl at full force, knocking her to the ground. The girl cried out, but Simle could not tell if it was in pain or surprise. Simle clamped her mouth around the girl's long black braids and the back of her robe. The girl beat Simle with her fists but it had no more effect on the dragon than a gnat would. Arrows clattered against her back, making Simle very glad she had tucked in her wings. She would have to spread them soon, though.

Simle ran to the clearing as swiftly as she could with a human clamped in her mouth. The girl wasn't too heavy, but she was bulky and certainly not cooperating. The trees opened up above her. Knowing that the humans might have kept up with her, Simle took a chance. She spread her wings, leaped mightily with her back legs, and wrapped her front legs around the human as she took to the sky.

The human screamed, setting off a ringing in Simle's ears.

"Stop that," Simle mumbled through a mouthful of hair and cloth. "Or I drop you."

The girl quieted. Simle tightened her grip and pumped her wings, trying to gain distance from the ground. She would never get any answers if she were to drop the human. Simle still couldn't move her head much, but she managed a glance downward. The humans fired arrows at her, but they were out of range now. They might track her, though. They had already found her once. Simle studied the slopes of the mountain. There had to be a cave somewhere.

Flying toward a high cliff, Simle spotted a crevice that could only mean one thing: a dragon's lair. She hoped whatever dragon might call it home wasn't around, because she needed it right now. Simle flew to the crevice and landed on the rocky ledge, careful not to let the human go. Unless this human possessed the gift of flight, there was no escape. The dragon lair entrance sat back from the ledge by perhaps ten or fifteen feet, giving enough of a flat surface that Simle could land and put the human down.

Simle said to the human, "I am going to let you go. There is no way down other than if I take you myself. Do you understand?"

The human nodded, or at least, Simle thought it was a nod. She wasn't sure if nodding meant the same thing for humans as it did for dragons. "Speak!" she barked, worried that the human couldn't understand her.

The human whispered, "Yes."

Simle spat out the girl's hair and robes. The girl

scrambled away from her in the wrong direction, almost to the cliff edge.

"Be careful!" Simle warned. The human looked behind her at the long drop, shuddered, and moved to huddle against the cliff wall, as far from both the lip of the cliff and Simle as she could manage in that small space. Simle guessed that she couldn't see the dragon lair entrance, for it was hidden behind a spindly tree and a lip of stone wall. Simle casually moved to block the girl's view of the wall, so she couldn't move past.

The girl just watched Simle, fear in her eyes. Even stronger than the fear, that hatred still burned there too. The jewel that had so confused Simle glittered at the girl's throat.

"Why did you take me?" the girl asked suddenly. Her eyes darted past Simle, looking more suspicious.

"Why did you want to capture me?" Simle retorted.

"Because you're a dragon," the girl spat. "Therefore you're my enemy!"

Simle glared at the girl and snapped, "Well, at least we agree on one thing!"

CHAPTER SEVEN

Tatelyn had never been so scared and angry in her entire life. Not only had their plan to capture the dragon failed, but she was now a captive herself. For some reason, though, the dragon seemed to have no interest in killing her—at least not yet. What other plans might it have, though? Tatelyn shuddered and wished she could see a way down off this mountaintop.

The dragon settled in to her spot on the small ledge, suddenly relaxing. "Who are you?" it asked, as though she were a fellow cleric meeting Tatelyn for the first time. Though perhaps not so polite. Tatelyn gaped.

"I know humans are mean and stupid and cruel. Rudeness should not surprise me," the dragon said when Tatelyn didn't answer. "Who are you?"

Tatelyn folded her arms across her chest. "Tatelyn of Forestedge," she said. "Not that it's any of your business."

"I am Simle," the dragon replied. "And who you are

74

most certainly is my business." Simle looked at her claws as though annoyed at how tiny they were. She gestured to Tatelyn's throat. "Where did you get that necklace?"

Tatelyn could not have been more surprised. That was a question Ramma would ask, not a savage creature. Next, would the dragon ask how she braided her hair?

"None of your concern," Tatelyn said, tucking the jewel under her robe. "Unless you're planning on stealing it to add to your treasure hoard."

The dragon snorted. "My kind does not care for sparkly gems. Coral and pearls are the only items of real value." The dragon's eyes glittered with what Tatelyn thought, for a moment, might be tears. But that was absurd. These creatures had no emotions.

The dragon was indeed crying, however. In fact, she was hunkering down for what looked like a good cry indeed. Tatelyn scooched back as far as she could without falling off the cliff to avoid the dragon's tears sizzling on the stone. They must be acidic, Tatelyn realized. How fitting. Everything about these creatures had the power to harm.

Once again Tatelyn glanced over the edge and was instantly dizzy from the steep carpet of green treetops. There was no escaping that way, unless she wanted to fall and roll all the way back to Forestedge. She couldn't see the town from here, which made her even more nervous.

Which direction was it—far below, hidden by the trees? Or on the other side of the mountain?

The dragon was still weeping. That made Tatelyn even angrier. "Stop it!" Tatelyn yelled. "How dare you cry? I'm the one who should be crying! My brother was killed by a copper dragon like you!"

The dragon's tears slowed and it glared at Tatelyn. "I am not copper! I'm bronze! The very idea! Copper dragons live in the mountains, and eat scorpions, and bre—"

"I don't care! You're a dragon!" Tatelyn sat down on the rocks. "Oh, why did you have to come here? Why can't you all just go away and leave us alone?"

"I would like nothing better!" the dragon roared. "I hate it here!"

Tatelyn blinked, startled.

"I want to go back to the Dragon Isles," the dragon continued, sitting up proudly. "I never wanted to come here, but my parents made me."

Dragons had parents? The thought had never occurred to Tatelyn, but of course, they must have. Where else would little dragons come from? Then another thought crossed her mind, far more chilling. What if the dragon's parents were around here as well?

"Wh-where are your parents?" Tatelyn asked, trying to keep the question casual.

Tears welled up in the dragon's eyes again. "My mother

was wounded in a fight. Fighting to protect humans! To protect you!"

"Don't cry again! You'll eat away the whole ledge!" Tatelyn said. She couldn't get any farther away, so instead she leaped up to rush toward the dragon, but she tripped and avoided falling in a puddle of acidic tears by inches. "A dragon never protected me! Never!"

"Then where did you get that necklace?" the dragon asked, pointing a finger at Tatelyn's neck. Tatelyn looked down and picked up the medallion of Mishakal. "Not that one," the dragon snapped. "The jewel. The one that matches this!"

Simle flipped her head to the side and a fine chain slithered around her neck. On the end of the chain, previously tucked behind the dragon's wings, was a pendant that matched the one Elistan had given Tatelyn.

"Where did you get that?" Tatelyn rose to her feet and took a step forward, her curiosity outweighing her fear of the dragon for a moment.

"My mother brought it home after protecting humans. You must have seen her if you have the other half."

The other half? Tatelyn looked closer and realized that, indeed, the pendant would fit together with hers. She shook her head slowly. "You are the first copper dragon I've seen since—"

"How many times must I tell you, I am not copper,

I'm BRONZE!" With the last word, the dragon flapped her wings.

"You're going to kill us both!" Tatelyn yelled. She edged away until her back was against the steep rock wall, and glanced up. Only a gifted climber could scale that. Her rage at being kidnapped, at dragons, at everything that had happened in the last few days bubbled up again. "I don't care what metal you are!" she shouted. "I didn't get this from a dragon. I haven't *seen* a dragon other than you for a year! And, may I say, it wasn't a good encounter then, either."

The dragon's raised wings drooped like a yellow flower wilting in the sun. "You didn't see my mother?" it whispered.

"No," Tatelyn said, feeling slightly sorry for the dragon. She beat the feeling down. But curiosity about the similar jewel won out over her anger for a moment. "May I look closer at the necklace?"

The dragon said nothing, but merely nodded. Tatelyn came closer, closer. What if it was a trap? But the dragon could have killed her by now, she realized, if that was its purpose. It must have been genuinely curious about her necklace.

Tatelyn took the dragon's pendant in one hand. Like hers, it was jagged along one edge. She took her pendant in the other hand and fitted them together like pieces of a jigsaw puzzle.

For a moment, she saw the completed star that the two pieces made. Then there was a brilliant flash of multicolored light and a roaring boom that shook rocks loose from the cliff. Tatelyn let go of the dragon's necklace as the force from the flash knocked her back into the scraggly tree, where she ducked for cover. Simle tucked her head and wings in until she resembled a ball.

The two waited for the rain of rocks to cease, then they peered at each other. That crafty dragon had done something, using the matching jewel as bait.

"What did you do?" Tatelyn shouted. A stray rock bounced down the cliff. Tatelyn ducked aside and it continued its fall down the mountain. "What did you do?"

"What did *I* do?" The dragon stood, craning her long neck to look at the new formations in the rock above them. "What did *you* do?"

"It was you! It had to be! You attacked my friends yesterday, and now—"

"They attacked me!" Simle stiffened. "I was just flying over and they attacked me! I defended myself!"

"You can't blame them," Tatelyn said, although now that Simle mentioned it, her friends never had said that the dragon threatened them first. "A copper dragon attacked this village not long ago."

"I am NOT a copper dragon!" This time the dragon roared so loudly that Tatelyn's ears rang with the sound.

"Your village must have done something to the copper dragon first!"

"We never did anything to that dragon," Tatelyn yelled. This dragon was really infuriating. How dare it suggest that Forestedge had done a single thing to bring on such an attack! "We only want the dragons to leave Krynn."

"Show me the way out and I'll go!" Simle shouted. Then she took a deep breath. Tatelyn braced herself for another attack of stench, but no foul air came forth. Simle appeared only to have been calming herself.

"It was the necklace that did that, it had to be," Simle said after a moment. "I know nothing of mine, only that my mother got it from some humans. Where did yours come from?"

If the dragon did have something to do with that flash, Tatelyn realized, she was one great actor. Dragons could be tricky, but she would get nowhere by continuing to accuse it. Certainly she wouldn't be getting off this cliff without trying to ameliorate whatever problem the dragon thought she had with Tatelyn. "It was given to me by a great leader," she told Simle. "I believe he thought it would help me and my friends with our goal."

"Which is?" Simle asked.

"Ridding Krynn of all dragons. Somehow convincing the people of Krynn that we were better off without them and finding a way to banish them."

"No argument here," Simle said. "Although I will leave long before you banish us. Why would your leader think it would help you?"

"Why should I tell you?" Tatelyn narrowed her eyes. The two stared at each other for so long that Tatelyn's eyes blurred at the edges, but she wouldn't be the one to look away first.

So she was taken by surprise when Simle grabbed her by the ankles and held her upside down over the edge of the cliff. Tatelyn screamed. The trees below her grew at impossibly steep angles for miles. Tatelyn had only the presence of mind to grab her necklace before it slipped up over her head, but she could do nothing about how her robes fell up around her head.

"Tell me," Simle growled. "You are nothing to me but another human. I have no problem with dropping you." The dragon stumbled a bit, making Tatelyn sway. If the dragon kept this up, Tatelyn was sure she would either sick up or faint.

Tatelyn wanted to hold out, but seeing the sheer drop below filled her mind with even more terror. "Put me down! Put me down!" she shrieked. Had she been thinking straight she wouldn't have been proud of her behavior, but that that moment, she didn't care. "All right!" Tatelyn cried. She was now more afraid than angry and didn't like it one bit. "I'll tell! Just please put me down!"

The dragon's grip shifted. For one horrifying moment, Tatelyn was sure the dragon was going to drop her into that forest below, which was filled with tree limbs and sharp rocks. Her eyes focused on a small, wandering line through the trees. Was it a path?

Suddenly she was flipping over, and she was sure the dragon had dropped her. "Aa-a-a-a-ai-i-i-i-i!" Tatelyn screamed. But then she felt firm ground under her feet. She collapsed, near tears. The dragon had been picking her *up*.

"So tell," Simle said flatly, crossing her scaly arms.

"Elistan told me this jewel belonged to Huma," Tatelyn said as she slyly peeked over the edge. Had she really seen a trail? Could she get to it?

"Never heard of either of them," Simle retorted, shaking her head as though recovering from a dizzy spell.

"Huma is a hero among humans, a knight who saved Krynn many, many years ago," Tatelyn said. "He drove the Dark Queen from this world, and with her, all dragons—good and evil."

"So he's the one," Simle said. "I must remember to thank him. What did he say that the good dragons did to him?"

Tatelyn thought. She realized uneasily that she never knew why the good dragons were banished along with the bad. She made up an answer that sounded good.

"Because dragons do not belong on Krynn. Black, gold, red, copper. They're all the same. Humans and dragons cannot coexist."

"Do you think I want to be here?" Simle roared. "Humans stole my siblings! They never did anything to you!"

"I didn't steal them!" Tatelyn yelled. "My brother didn't steal them either! No one from Forestedge ever stole a dragon egg!"

"And no bronze dragon ever attacked a human without provocation! Bronzes love humans—although why, I'll never know. But it was humans who took all the dragon eggs." Simle opened her mouth as if to say more, but tears welled in her eyes. She blinked them away, but they kept coming. When she rubbed at her eyes with one bronze claw, Tatelyn bolted for the cliff edge behind her and stepped over it.

The ground was still steep here, but it wasn't the sheer drop that bordered the ledge on the other sides. Tatelyn fell a few feet, bracing herself for a painful landing. There was a jolt as she landed on a dirt path, but no pain. The dragon roared above her, and Tatelyn quickly got to her feet. The trail ran both up and down the mountain, but there was only one way Tatelyn wanted to go. She half ran, half stumbled down the path. Above her, she could hear the dragon spread its wings and take to the air. Were the trees thick enough to hide her?

As she dared a glance behind her, Tatelyn tripped over a root and went sprawling. Her hands struck the path and pebbles and grit ground into her skin. She was too scared to feel pain, though, and she scrambled to her feet yet again. The dragon roared again, this time much closer. Tatelyn's fear must have blinded her, because she didn't see the drop. After a few more steps, suddenly the path fell away beneath her feet and she was running in midair. Tatelyn had a brief glimpse of jagged rocks below, trees crushed beneath them. They must be the boulders that fell from the cliff earlier, she thought with an odd detachment as she fell toward them. But then she was rising rather than falling, the boulders and trees far below receding even farther away beneath her feet. Simle's claws were around Tatelyn's shoulders, holding her tightly but not hurting.

The dragon flew up, up, up, and with a lack of grace Tatelyn didn't expect from a dragon, hit her head on the rock overhanging the cliff Tatelyn had just jumped from. Tatelyn felt a sharp ache in her head as the dragon suddenly dropped her on the rock ledge once more.

Simle whimpered. This startled Tatelyn—that sound was not the reaction she expected. The dragon should have been angry that she tried to escape, but instead Simle looked as though she was hurt.

Tatelyn sympathized. Her head ached dreadfully, and although her scraped palms did not sting yet, they would soon. She needed to clean out these wounds and heal them before that happened. Mishakal, Tatelyn prayed silently, one of your devoted servants is in need. Please take my pain away. Tatelyn waited for the familiar feeling of peace and healing, but it did not come. Frowning, Tatelyn clasped her medallion and and prayed once more. Nothing. Her palms were just as scraped up as before. It would really hurt to scrub out that gravel.

"What did you do now?" she yelled at the dragon, who was cradling her own front claws. As she turned her head to look at Tatelyn, the pain in Tatelyn's head worsened.

"What did *I* do?" the dragon whispered, as though she, too, was in horrible pain.

Tatelyn got to her feet and stumbled toward Simle. "What did you—" Tatelyn's accusation was lost as she tripped on a loose stone. She fell to the ground, scraping her hands yet again, but not feeling a thing.

Simle roared. Tatelyn thought the dragon was trying to frighten her, but she wasn't even looking at her. Instead, Simle was looking at her palms.

"What did you do to me, human?" the dragon asked. Tatelyn got to her feet and walked closer. A cut on the dragon's head trickled green blood. That must have happened when Simle hit her head on the cliff.

Tatelyn looked at her scraped hands. Even with a delayed reaction, her palms should have felt as if they were on fire by now, judging from the damage. Yet she felt nothing. She poked one scraped palm with her forefinger. No pain. She rubbed at a bit of rock that had slipped under a layer of skin. There was pressure from her finger and the rock, but no pain at all.

"Does your head hurt?" Tatelyn asked Simle.

"No, but my hands! They sting! I've never felt anything like it." A bit of blood trickled into Simle's right eye. She blinked, wiping it away. "Where did that come from?" she asked, looking at the blood on her claw.

"You have a bad cut on your head."

"I don't feel anything," Simle said. "How strange . . ." Simle stopped and looked at Tatelyn. "Let me see your hands."

Tatelyn held out her hands, palms facing the dragon. Simle gasped. She looked up at the rock she'd bumped, which was covered in blood from her head wound, then back to Tatelyn, raising a claw. Tatelyn stepped back, thinking her throat was about to be slit. But all Simle did was close her eyes tightly and thrust the claw into the soft flesh under her front leg.

It was as if a long steel knife had stabbed Tatelyn under her left arm. Tatelyn cried out and grabbed her armpit. Yet despite the horrible agony, Tatelyn could tell there was no physical damage to her body there. No bleeding, no tear in the fabric of her robe.

Simle and Tatelyn gaped at each other. As if with one voice, they both asked, "What did you do to me?"

CHAPTER EIGHT

lood trickled down Simle's cheek and dripped on the rock below her, but she felt no pain at all in her head. She looked up at the rock ledge. There was matching green blood there where she had hit her head. Green, not red. The collision had been bad, yet she felt no pain on her head. Her claws, however, felt as though they had been torn off with excruciating slowness. Yet they looked whole. Perfect, in fact.

Simle looked at the human girl before her on the rocks, the girl whose hands were so scraped up, yet did not appear to pain her. Tatelyn kept putting her hands to her head as though it pained her instead. Simle felt dazed more from wonder than from pain. Could it be possible?

"Am I feeling your pain?" Simle asked hesitantly.

"I . . . I think you are," Tatelyn replied, looking as dazed from the concept as the pain. "As I feel yours."

"Did you do this?" Simle asked. Tatelyn shook her head so hard Simle felt a bit of vertigo. In that instant, Simle knew why she had felt dizzy when she was holding the girl over the cliff edge. She sighed. "I was afraid not. I thought so at first but . . ." Simle stared at the jewel around Tatelyn's neck, then looked at the one around her own neck. "Do you think you putting the pendant together caused this?"

"I'm just an acolyte. I know precious little of magic besides praying for healing to my god, Mishakal. But I think it's possible the jewels could have caused this," Tatelyn said, getting to her feet. Simle winced as the girl put weight on the scrapes, but managed to keep from yelling. She felt silly yelping about all these injuries that, even by human standards, seemed very minor. "You are a cleric. Is there anything you can do for your hands? Or my head?" Simle asked.

"I tried healing myself earlier, but it didn't work. Let me try healing you." Tatelyn motioned with one raw hand. Simle lowered her head to Tatelyn's level. The girl cupped the Bronze's head in both hands and whispered a prayer.

Nothing.

Tatelyn bit her lip, looking at the dragon's wound and her scraped palms. "I need to do something. If I can't heal us, perhaps I can find some herbs and make a poultice."

"The pain doesn't bother me," Simle said, hiding yet another wince as Tatelyn poked curiously at her hand. "I'm not some feeble human."

"Just because you can't feel it doesn't mean that cut isn't serious. Even mine could be bad if they fester," Tatelyn argued. "I know of some plants that will help, if we can find them."

Simle remembered some of the plants the healer had brought to treat her mother. Mother. This time Simle winced, but not from physical pain. The girl was right.

"Where would these plants grow?"

"Not up here," Tatelyn said. "Closer to the ground. Near water would be best."

Simle narrowed her eyes at the girl. "You'll try to escape again."

"I can't," Tatelyn said flatly. "If we're connected like this, running away would do me no good. And if we aren't connected, why do you need me? I already told you I don't know anything about who hurt your mother."

Simle sighed. Maybe the girl had told her all she knew of the pendant, maybe not. But they wouldn't solve whatever had been caused by that flash of light by standing up here talking. She would keep a close eye on Tatelyn, in case she did try to escape again.

"Wonderful. Let's go." Simle knelt down before Tatelyn. The girl would have to climb, but she could reach the top of Simle's back easily.

"Wait!" Tatelyn exclaimed, taking a few steps back. "We're flying?"

"How else can we get there?" Simle asked. "That path you found ended badly. This is the quickest way." Really, these humans were silly creatures. It's amazing that they survived this long. And so fragile! Simle looked in disgust at the wounds on the human's hands. It had taken a very heavy and very sharp rock to hurt Simle's head, yet this creature could damage itself merely by falling.

Tatelyn still looked uncertain, but she climbed up onto Simle's back and sat down between her wings, wrapping her small legs around the dragon's neck. Simle moved her wings experimentally.

"Can you stay on?" Simle really didn't care if the human fell off her back, but what would happen if the human was killed? Would Simle feel that pain? Would she die? That was a disturbing notion.

"I think so," Tatelyn said. Reaching down behind her, Tatelyn grabbed the base of Simle's wings and held tight. "Can you still fly?"

"I won't know until I try." Simle turned about swiftly and ran to the edge of the cliff, spreading her wings wide and leaping into the air. As she left the ground, Simle had a single panicked thought: What if I can't fly?

The next moment proved this worry unfounded. Simle glided through the air easily. She could tell from the weight that the human girl was still holding on tight. She shook slightly, but that did not affect Simle's flying.

Before long, Simle began to feel sick to her stomach, like the time she had eaten a rotten piece of kelp as a wyrmling. The ground below her spun slightly. What was happening? Was this part of the spell?

Tatelyn screamed. Simle looked up and saw a large tree looming before them. She banked sharply upward and to the right, narrowly missing it, then dived down on the other side. As Simle pulled up out of the dive, the world went black. Simle gasped, but before she could begin to panic, her vision was back.

I can't fly like this, Simle thought. Scanning the ground below, she spied a large meadow and landed as quickly as possible. Tatelyn either hopped or fell off, but Simle barely noticed. The dragon retched into the grasses while Tatelyn watched her with a disgusted expression.

"What happened?" Tatelyn asked when Simle finished emptying her stomach of her last meal.

"I don't know," Simle said weakly. "I've never felt like that before. I feel sick to my stomach, and dizzy, and for a moment I couldn't see."

"Sick and dizzy? That was how I felt when you flew me up to the cliff." Tatelyn snapped her fingers and once again, Simle felt the pain as the girl's finger hit her scraped palm. "You now react to heights the way I do!"

The girl was right. Simle recalled the odd moment of dizziness she had when suspending the girl over the cliff edge. "I can't fly?" Simle would have roared, but feared the fish she ate before the animal would swim up her throat and out her mouth. "We have to figure out how to break this spell!"

"First let me see what I can do for our wounds," Tatelyn said firmly.

Simle kept a close eye on the girl as she wandered about the meadow examining flowers. Near a small stream, Tatelyn found a cluster of white blossoms. She gathered them up in her robes and carried them back to Simle, then mashed the flowers to a pulp between two rocks as Simle watched over her shoulder. Tatelyn then set the pulp aside and held the hem of her blue robe up to Simle.

"Can you tear this?" she asked. Simle had no idea what the girl was doing, but she slit the hem neatly with one sharp claw. Tatelyn spread the mashed flowers on the cloth, then held it up to Simle.

"Bend down," Tatelyn said. Simle did so and Tatelyn tied the cloth around her head.

"I don't feel anything different," Simle said.

"I do," Tatelyn said, putting more flower pulp on the rest of the hem. She tied it over one hand, and in her own hands Simle felt first a sting, then cooling relief.

"It's working!" Simle exclaimed. Perhaps humans were not useless after all. Tatelyn did the same for her other hand, and the same relief spread through Simle's other hand.

"Now that that's done," Tatelyn said, fiddling with one of her braids, "How can we undo this spell?"

The human was right. For every spell, there was a counterspell. But who would know it? "What of this human who gave you your jewel?"

"Elistan," Tatelyn breathed. "He's head of the church of Paladine and a very wise man. If anyone will know, he will. Even if he doesn't, surely he would know someone who could help us. But I don't want to bring a dragon to Palanthas, even if most people there do revere you."

"They revere us?" Simle asked, both shocked and pleased.

"Not all. But most. The good dragons supposedly saved the city during the war. It doesn't matter. I won't take you there."

"Would you prefer to come to my home?" Simle asked acidly. "My mother and father are there, as well as my uncle. I'm sure they would love to see you."

Tatelyn blanched, as Simle guessed she would. Simle's family would never harm the girl, despite how frustrating she was. They'd probably throw her a party. In any case, Simle did not want any humans around her family again, ever.

"Anyway," Simle said, "my mother can't tell us anything. She's very ill and . . ." Simle turned away, blinking back tears.

Tatelyn turned away and said, "Fine. We'll go to Palanthas." She looked at the sun, which was approaching its noon zenith, and the mountains behind her. "We're on the other side of the mountains where you kidnapped me, aren't we?" she asked.

Simle glared and nodded. She had done that on purpose, to put some distance between Tatelyn and her friends.

Tatelyn got her bearings and began walking swiftly north. Simle followed her, but her legs felt heavy and her whole body dragged. "Wait!" Simle said, then gasped in shock at herself. Was she actually having trouble keeping up with a human?

The two of them continued in silence for a long time. They passed through forests and meadows, and went up steep trails and down rocky ravines. Even though Simle was unused to walking for such a long distance, she was surprised at how quickly she grew tired. By contrast, Tatelyn practically skipped ahead of her. The magic must also have switched their basic energy. Tatelyn now had the typical stamina of a dragon, while Simle was stuck with the puny constitution of a human.

"When I find who is responsible for this," Simle grumbled, "I am going to bite their head off. I don't care if it's a human or a dragon." She snorted—and realized something was wrong. Where was the lightning that normally accompanied snorts? Horrible realization crept over Simle. She turned her head away from Tatelyn and tried to breathe out noxious fumes.

Nothing came out but air. My weapons are gone, Simle thought. All I have now are my teeth, claws, and tail. She looked at Tatelyn moving swiftly ahead. I won't tell her, she decided. Let her think I'm still dangerous.

As the trail changed from easy, flat land to another incline, Simle slowed even more. She wasn't sure she could make it, but she didn't want the human to know about her weakness. Tatelyn paused and turned back to look at Simle lagging behind. "Come on, slowpoke," she called. "We can cover more ground before nightfall!"

Looking up again at the incline, Simle gave in. She had to admit she was exhausted. "It's your fault I'm slow," Simle said. "I must have your energy."

"No wonder," Tatelyn said. "I feel like I could walk all the way to Palanthas and back in a day!"

"Well, I don't," Simle said. "And if we hadn't been switched, you wouldn't be able to either. So quit running ahead!"

Tatelyn grinned. "Why don't we stop for the evening? I can build a fire. Can you find us something to eat?"

"Why me? Can't humans hunt?" Simle asked. Better to taunt the human than admit she was too tired to even venture into the nearby trees. "And why do we need a fire?"

"For warmth and cooking."

"Cooking? You mean food?" Simle shuddered. "How horrible." Still, the thought of food made Simle's stomach twist painfully. She had none of the gurgles of hunger, but she felt the pain of an empty stomach. She heard Tatelyn's belly rumble loudly. When had the girl last eaten?

"Just find us something," Tatelyn said. "You might as well put those teeth and claws to some good use. I'll find firewood." Tatelyn wandered into a dense thicket where the underbrush hid several broken tree limbs.

As soon as she was out of sight, Simle tried to polymorph into a squirrel. Nothing. She tried a few other animals, all with the same lack of result. Her magic was gone, just as the girl's clerical powers were.

Another stab of hunger made Simle forget the loss of her magic. If she could find water, she could find enough fish for her and the annoying human. As tempting as it was to let Tatelyn starve, Simle did not look forward to feeling someone else's hunger—hunger that she could not diminish by eating. Far off, she heard the rushing water of a large river, perhaps the one in which she had slept the previous night.

As Simle walked toward the water, every bone and muscle in her body ached from the exertion the human felt from this very long, exhausting day. What if they never fixed this? Tatelyn would reap all the benefits of being a dragon, while Simle stayed trapped with the fragility of a human. No magic, no flying, no transforming. If they didn't fix it soon, Simle feared they might have to stick together for a long time to come.

CHAPTER NINE

If Tatelyn had not been so enthusiastic about her new-found ability to walk for long distances and not tire a bit, she might have heard the crackle of twigs behind her. As it was, she had no idea she was not alone until something grabbed her from behind and pulled a rough sack over her head. She cried out once, but her captor gagged her. Her hands were bound as well, but her feet were left free. She kicked out and heard a low grunt. Her captor yanked the rope tying her hands, making her stumble forward.

"No more of that," said a harsh voice. "You're coming with me, girl." The owner of the voice yanked the rope again, and Tatelyn had no choice but to follow blindly, her heart thudding madly. Who was her captor? What did he want with her? She knew it was a male from the low voice, but more than that she couldn't say.

They walked for a long while. The grass began to thin and give way to moss as they traveled deeper into the forest. She couldn't tell what direction they traveled, except that the terrain wasn't so harsh as the way she and Simle had come. Tatelyn wondered if the rope was cutting into her wrists at all. Perhaps Simle would feel the pain and come to her rescue.

"What do you have there, Humtak?" a new voice barked. "Dinner?"

"A girl. Must be from the village. I thought she could provide us with information."

"A good idea. How unlike you, Humtak." More voices laughed, sounding like rocks tumbling down a hill. How many were there? At least three, Tatelyn decided. She was outnumbered.

"Shall we question her now?" Humtak asked, bringing Tatelyn closer to the voices. She felt the heat of a nearby fire, smelled food roasting. Her stomach growled again, though she didn't feel any hunger.

"Not until Numt returns, Humtak. You know he likes to be present for every, ahem, interrogation."

"What do we do with her until then?"

"Put her to sleep, of course!" A heavy object hit Tatelyn in the head. She felt nothing, but the force knocked her to the ground. She lay there motionless. They must have expected the blow to knock her out. If she pretended to be unconscious, perhaps she could learn something. Hopefully that one blow was not enough to put Simle out for very long.

The rope tugged again, but not much. Humtak or

one of the others must have tied her to something—a tree, perhaps. Tatelyn could hear the faint calls of owls, the chattering of squirrels. Were any of them Simle? For a moment a shining flash of hope brightened Tatelyn's thoughts. The dragon could transform herself . . . unless her magic was as lost as Tatelyn's clerical powers. Tatelyn's shoulders drooped in disappointment before she could control the reaction.

"Are you sure she's out? She shouldn't overhear our plans."

A hard object hit Tatelyn in the stomach. For once the lack of pain seemed to be a good thing—she had no trouble pretending to be out cold. A sharp rock poked into her cheek. Good. That was yet another pain that Simle might feel and realize the danger Tatelyn was in.

"She's out," grunted Humtak. "We'll wake her up when Numt returns."

"I just hope she has some useful information," one of the others said, his voice receding as they walked away. "Who would have expected one of the town whelps to be running around loose this late at night?"

"The Dark Queen is giving us good fortune indeed," said the first voice.

The Dark Queen? Takhisis! The evil goddess directly opposed Mishakal and had been responsible for starting the War of the Lance a few years ago. If these creatures looked to Takhisis for good fortune, they could not possibly be good. Tatelyn's brain neared blind panic and she fought to remain logical. If she was someone like Elrit, she could pretend to be sympathetic to Takhisis. But if these guys were the least bit observant, they would have noticed Tatelyn's blue robes and medallion of Mishakal and known immediately that she was no ally.

It sounded as though there were indeed three of them, not counting the missing Numt. Tatelyn prayed to Mishakal that Numt would stay away a good, long while. She did not know if her prayers would be answered anymore, but the habit was so deeply ingrained that she could not go without at least asking the goddess for help.

"Just think of the status the treasure will bring us, Ventur!" said Humtak with a slurp that sounded like eating.

Treasure? In the forest? Tatelyn wanted to hear more, but a new voice entered the conversation.

"What is this? Where did you get that human?"

"She was just wandering about the forest, Numt," Humtak answered. "Silly thing. One never knows what evil beasties might be about." The group chuckled harshly.

"Quite right," Numt said. Tatelyn heard his steps approach the fire, where the others had been eating. She concentrated on staying as still as possible. "Have you discovered anything from interrogating her?" Numt asked, chewing loudly. Tatelyn tried to keep from shuddering. What was he planning for her?

"Nothing. We thought you would want to be here for the questioning," Humtak said.

"I certainly do," Numt said. He turned from the fire and walked over to Tatelyn. "Wake up!" Numt said, slapping Tatelyn's face through the sack. She felt the force of the blow, but not the tiniest whisper of pain. There was something else about the hand that struck her too. Devoid of pain, she found that she was able to feel more of what touched her. It had not been skin that struck her face. Gloves, perhaps?

The others were untying her now. What were they going to do? One of them ripped the sack from her head and Tatelyn was momentarily blinded by the leaping fire, which was almost touching the trees overhanging the crude camp. There were no tents, but a stewpot simmered over the fire. From the smell, Tatelyn didn't want to know what their dinner was. As her eyes adjusted, Tatelyn got her first good look at her captors. They were not human, elf, or even ogre or goblin. These were forms that she had never seen before, but had heard tales of many, many times.

Draconians.

Tatelyn swallowed a scream. While her nightmares were filled with real dragons, there were other creatures that walked the edges of her mind during sleep: Humans that suddenly took on the forms of dragons, twisted and perverted into the creatures she hated. If she could feel pain, Tatelyn thought, she would pinch herself and wake from this nightmare. But she was awake, being shoved to her feet by these true-life monsters.

Tatelyn didn't know which kind of draconians these were—there were as many kinds of draconians as there were good dragons, whose eggs were corrupted to make these brutes—but they all appeared to be the same color and size, whatever they were. They were easily as tall as Rogan, with large wings and bronze-tinged scales that reminded her horribly of Simle. All four were dressed in dark, blood-splattered plate armor. In their clawed hands each one of them held a weapon, but the weapons were not what frightened Tatelyn the most. After all, none of them could make her feel the least bit of pain.

No, the alarm that shot through her at seeing the draconians who were now dragging her to the fire was from a cause even more dire: How would she know if her arm got broken or if she got a deadly wound? That complication had not occurred to her before.

Completely devoid of any emotion save malice, the draconians ringed Tatelyn as if they were evil fireflies. Numt stepped forward, raising his weapon. Tongs. Although Tatelyn kept telling herself that she would feel no pain, she could not control the sinking feeling in her stomach. What was he going to do to her?

The tongs came nearer and nearer to Tatelyn's face. She nearly went cross-eyed focusing on them. Numt held them a hairsbreadth from her nose.

They obviously wanted something from her, or she would be dead already. But what information could she possibly give? Perhaps they were going to attack Forestedge. How long would it take them to get there from here? It would have taken her days to get to this side of the mountain had she not taken a dragon shortcut over it. How fast could draconians travel? All Tatelyn could see were the red-hot tongs glowing in front of her face, singeing the air and quite possibly her skin. It was all she could do not to scream, though she couldn't help letting a whimper escape. But after a few more moments of silent fear, Numt put the tongs back in the fire.

"So, little one, you fear us," he said. "As well you should. However, I am somewhat of a sentimentalist. I don't like torturing young, pretty girls."

"No, not at all," Ventur said with a chuckle. He flung the dagger into the ground a foot or so from where Tatelyn stood. Then he retrieved it and flung it again, aiming it closer to Tatelyn, and repeated the action again and again, coming closer and closer to her as Numt continued to talk. His toothy smile and pointy scales made him look like a human with a dragon head, and it was almost impossible for Tatelyn to concentrate on what Numt was saying.

"However," Numt continued, and Tatelyn was sure she'd missed something, "if you are *not* hospitable and do *not* tell us about this fine land we visit and the town we seek, perhaps we might have to do some things to you that are not so pleasant."

Tatelyn's mind raced. She could not tell them about Forestedge; the town had just begun to repair itself. But what would the draconians do to her? While she couldn't feel pain, she was certain that her body could only withstand so much abuse before she died, especially since she could no longer heal herself.

As if reading her mind, Numt said, "You wear the robes of a cleric of Mishakal. Curious that nothing happened to me when I did this." He reached a claw toward Tatelyn's neck. Tatelyn braced herself for what must surely be coming, but no shock issued forth from the necklace. Numt stood close enough to kiss, his bronze claw wrapped around the medallion, but showed no sign of pain.

"I believe you are a false cleric," he declared. "I believe you donned the medallion and robes of a cleric, but are no such thing."

Tatelyn thought fast. "There was a play in town."

The draconian nodded. "Perhaps. Perhaps not. In any case, you do not have the defenses that my men and

I initially thought you had. And no one is coming to your rescue. We certainly can't let you go—you might reach your village first and raise the alarm."

Tatelyn shook her head, trying to look scared and hopeless, but at the same time her mind was putting pieces together. She was not alone in the forest. She had no idea how long she had been gone, but surely Simle was beginning to wonder. By now, the dragon probably thought Tatelyn had deserted her. Tatelyn would have thought so if Simle had wandered off and not returned. If Simle felt pain—Tatelyn's pain— she should be on her way in this direction. Tatelyn knew what she needed to do.

"Tell us a bit about your town," Numt said. "How are the defenses?"

"We have a garrison of Solamnic Knights at our beck and call," Tatelyn said glibly. "Years ago, one of the villagers saved the life of a noble child who wandered off during a hunt, and ever since then, they have defended our village with their lives."

"Did you hear that, Numt?" Ventur gasped. "Knights! Maybe we should think twice about this."

"Fool, she's lying!" Numt snarled. He grabbed the tongs out of the fire and clamped them around Tatelyn's wrist. She felt pressure and intense heat, but no pain. Showing no pain was easy, but she had to pretend to endure the pain a little while longer. The sooner she cracked, the sooner the draconians would either cease their torture or kill her.

"How far is it to your village?" Numt asked.

"Only a few moments if you find the portal in the woods. That is how I came to be here."

This time none of the draconians bought her fib. Numt nodded to Ventur, who drew back his dagger and flung it toward Tatelyn. It buried itself in her right shoulder and blood began to trickle down her arm.

"How many live in your village?" Numt asked, releasing the tongs from her wrist and tossing them back into the fire.

"It varies between ten and ten thousand. People are always coming and going. They shall welcome you, and be even more thankful when you leave."

This time Numt did not even look at the other draconians before they advanced upon her. As Tatelyn saw the sword rise in the moonlight she prayed for three things: that Simle would find her swiftly, that the dragon would not be in too much pain to help, and that the draconians would not kill her before Simle could save her.

CHAPTER TEN

"Where is that human?" Simle grumbled. Tatelyn had left before the sun had fully set. Now darkness enveloped the forest, broken only by the slivers of light from the red and silver moons when they could be seen through the canopy of trees. Surely it did not take that long to gather wood for a fire.

Simle sighed, sure that Tatelyn had run off again. On top of all the other problems she had now, must she keep track of where the human was at all times? Simle looked at Solinari, the silver moon. She would wait until it was directly overhead, and then she would go in search for the human. She chuckled. All she would need to do to find the human was to hit herself a few times and follow the screams.

A sudden pain struck Simle's head. With the pain came elation. Has the spell been broken? Simle touched her head, still sticky with blood. But there was no tenderness when she touched the wound from this afternoon.

The curse must not have been undone after all—Tatelyn must have been hurt. Now she had to go find her.

Muttering a few choice epithets in Draconic about humans, she looked about the forest. The human had walked to the east, so Simle followed suit. She couldn't have gone too far, not as slowly as humans moved. Simle followed the girl's tracks, though perhaps not as well as she could have if she'd learned to track land creatures back when Uncle Nuvar had tried to teach her during one of his lectures on humans. She hadn't paid attention, declaring that she wanted nothing to do with land animals if they trafficked with humans.

But Simle had keen eyes and a sharp sense of smell, and she thought she was doing a pretty good job when the tracks suddenly ended at a patch of torn grass and a broken branch. There were other tracks here, tracks that didn't look human in origin. It looked like Tatelyn had been captured here, then dragged elsewhere. Much as the human annoyed Simle, she knew she had to find Tatelyn. If whatever took her was the thing that was hurting her, it could turn an already bad situation into a downright dangerous one.

A few bats flew overhead. Simle looked at them with envy. So many small creatures around her could fly, but she couldn't. She wasn't sure how flying would affect her if Tatelyn wasn't with her, but it seemed too risky to try.

The last thing she wanted was to crash while looking for that annoying human.

Small creatures! Perhaps one of them saw what happened to Tatelyn! Simle looked around for something small that was unlikely to have moved. She spotted a squirrel, looking much like Simle must have looked when she took that form, peering down from a tree.

"Excuse me," Simle asked. "Did you see a human here?"

The tiny animal did not answer, but cocked its head and twitched its tail. Simle sighed, blowing leaves about the creature. It chittered at her and darted into a hollow of the tree.

Foolish, Simle thought. Talking to other animals was part of her magic. She should have known. It wasn't like animals spoke a humanoid language like Common or Elvish.

She was truly alone and powerless in this world. Dragons weren't supposed to feel powerless. Despite her great size and sharp claws and teeth, she had no magic, no breath weapons, and no flying ability. Perhaps she could still fly if the human weren't on her back, getting sick from flying and making Simle feel it, but Simle didn't want to take the chance and possibly crash again.

Enough, Simle scolded herself, focusing on the torn grass and unfamiliar tracks. She still had her intelligence. Dragons were far smarter than humans, and she still had her eyes and nose. She would find that human. As much as she hated to admit it, she *had* to find Tatelyn.

The unfamiliar tracks beside Tatelyn's looked too large to be human, and besides, Simle was sure that if they were Tatelyn's friends, they'd have come charging back to capture Simle again. It was possible Tatelyn had been captured by goblins or ogres or some other creature. Just because humans thought they owned Krynn didn't mean they were the only inhabitants, even in this human-infested area, and the tracks looked too irregular to be clad in boots. There even appeared to be claws.

Despite her size, Simle found it was easy to walk in the forest. The tracks disappeared every so often as she passed rocky ground, but she always found them quickly again, mostly by the musky scent that accompanied the tracks. Perhaps tracking would not be that difficult, she thought, almost skipping ahead.

There was water nearby too, which served to further lighten her mood. She had been away from water too long. A nice dip would comfort her.

Simle followed the tracks to the bank of a stream. Bending her head, she drank deeply, not even noticing the lack of salt this time. After a good, long drink, she looked for the tracks on the opposite side. But Simle could find no more trace of the strange, clawed footprints for yards in either direction.

Simle sat down in the stream with a splash. These creatures were clever. They must have taken Tatelyn into the stream, but instead of going straight across, they had either gone up- or downstream. Which way, though?

Simle picked downstream and ambled that way, examining the shoreline carefully. There were no signs of tracks. Had she picked the wrong direction entirely? How much time had she wasted? Simle slapped her tail against the water, raising a large wave that rippled to the shores. If only she could fly or talk to the local animals! She would have found Tatelyn ages ago.

A sharp, burning pain encircled Simle's front leg. She roared and stuck her leg in the water as deep as it would go, but the pain didn't lessen. It felt as though someone had wrapped a white-hot band of iron around her scales.

Tatelyn! Simle realized, shaking her head. This was her pain, not Simle's. Where was she? Simle looked around, but the dark forest offered no clue to a direction. How could she possibly find Tatelyn?

As though answering Simle's question, a thin, far-off sound reached her ears. Still, it was familiar. She had heard that sound when she first captured Tatelyn—the girl was screaming again. This time, though, Tatelyn's screams were not of pain or fear, not the kind of pain Simle felt.

Tatelyn was screaming to show Simle her location. The human was not as stupid as Simle had thought!

Simle's first instinct was to crash through the woods at top speed in the direction of the cries, but she managed to check herself. Until she knew what held Tatelyn, she had to be stealthy.

She soon found the trail again, which was fortunate. As she got closer, she could hear voices as well as screams. She slowed her pace and snuck as quietly as she could through the forest, toward a fire flickering through the trees.

"Why won't you tell us what we need to know?" someone shouted with a harsh anger Simle wasn't sure she'd ever heard before. "If you'd just cooperate, we'd quit hurting you."

"I won't tell you anything about Forestedge," Tatelyn said. Her voice was still strong. "I won't help you harm my people."

There was silence, then laughter. "What do we want with Forestedge? We seek the treasure of Mountainhome."

"You fools! You captured someone from the wrong town!" exclaimed another voice. "What a waste of time!"

"She'll waste no more of it."

They were going to kill Tatelyn! Not that she cared for the human, but what would happen if Tatelyn died while they still felt each other's pain? With a roar, Simle broke from her hiding spot. There were four creatures there, one with a sword pointed at Tatelyn. Simle barreled into that creature and knocked it over, glancing at Tatelyn. There was blood on her head from a wound similar to the one Simle had sustained earlier, as well as a burn mark around one arm and blood running down her shoulder, which explained why Simle's shoulder ached. The shoulder worried Simle the most. She had to get Tatelyn out of there quickly before her captors could do any more damage.

Turning to face the creatures, Simle gasped.

Simle had seen many strange creatures since leaving her home, but she had never even heard of things such as this. They seemed to be some odd meld of human and lizard. They were about the size of large human males, but covered in metallic scales with clawed hands and long, sinuous tails—no human Simle had ever seen had a tail like that. Glittering intelligence shone in their eyes, framed by reptilian facial features. No, not reptile, Simle realized in horror, seeing their leathery wings. Dragon.

Somehow, someone had mixed dragon and human. Simle had no idea such an atrocity existed.

"Tell me where the nearest human village is and I will spare you," she said to the creatures. "This human is under my protection."

The creature Simle had knocked over got to his feet. The others looked to him, so he must have been their leader.

"It never ceases to amaze me. How can relatives of ours come to the defense of these sniveling humans?"

Simle was somewhat in agreement with the creature, but she had to protect Tatelyn. Her own life depended on it.

"Say," said one of the other creatures, peering closely at Simle. "That's one of our kin!"

Kin? Simle blinked at the creatures. What were they talking about?

The leader snorted and waved one clawed hand toward Simle. The others advanced toward Simle, weapons raised. Between their battered bits and pieces of armor and their beaten, well-sharpened swords, these creatures looked battle hardy.

With a swipe of one claw, Simle slit the ropes binding Tatelyn's feet and hands. She doubted the girl could fight, but at least she could pull herself out of harm's way. Meanwhile, Simle whipped her tail across the ground, tripping two of the creatures. The move surprised them and they had little time to recover. Then she leaped into the air and came down hard, snapping the neck of one creature. The body's skin crumbled to dust, leaving only a strange-looking skeleton.

The other three shouted and backed away. They were afraid of her. At last, someone was afraid of her! Simle roared in triumph. Then a strange vibration began at her feet. What on Krynn? Simle peered closer at the bones at her feet. They were the source of the vibration. Strange. She'd never heard of vibrating bones.

BANG!

The explosion flung Simle backward into a large pine. For a moment, Simle vaguely thought that perhaps she should have known better, but then for the first time that evening, Tatelyn screamed in genuine pain. It took Simle a moment to remember where she was. As she turned her head something caught her eye.

Crossing her eyes, she looked down her nose and gasped. Fragments of bone had stuck in her face. No wonder Tatelyn screamed! Simle couldn't tell how much damage had been done, but at least she could still see—fortunately none of the fragments had hit her eyes.

Where were her attackers? A few feet away, one of the creatures cradled an almost detached arm, cursing in pain. The leader, however, was still unharmed. It drew its sword and faced Simle.

"Foolish Bronze," the leader snarled. "Idealistic and foolhardy, like all our metallic cousins. Go ahead and fight me. But you've seen what happens when we die. For every one of us you kill, you face an explosion. You can't defeat us, not without harming your precious human."

Simle glanced back at Tatelyn. The girl was lying on the ground like a beached jellyfish, limp and curled. The pain in her eyes showed how bad Simle had been hurt in the explosion. When Simle turned back, the creatures were running into the forest. She resisted the urge to chase them and instead bent to Tatelyn.

"You're hurt." Simle could both see on Tatelyn and feel on her own body how much damage the creatures had done to the girl.

"I know nothing of healing humans," Simle said. "Where is the nearest human settlement?"

Tatelyn closed her eyes, thinking. "The draconians spoke of a town to the south," she whispered. "That's where they're going. We must warn them. There may be others."

"We have to save you," Simle said. "Can you climb on my back?"

Wincing, Tatelyn pushed herself to her feet as Simle lay down. Tatelyn climbed up and slumped against Simle's wings. Simle folded them over her in case the girl lost consciousness, then began to run southward as quickly as she could without risking Tatelyn falling off. As she ran, the word Tatelyn referred to the creatures with kept repeating in her head. What on Krynn was a "draconian"?

CHAPTER ELEVEN

Tatelyn drifted in and out of pain as Simle carried her away from the draconians' camp. She could see the blood on her shoulder and the charred skin on her wrist where the draconians had tortured her. Yet all the pain centered on her face, from the explosion that hit Simle. Hopefully there would be a cleric at Mountainhome who could help them.

Simle did not try to talk to Tatelyn as she ran. Tatelyn was very grateful for that small mercy, as she didn't have the energy to form words. She focused on trying to recall everything the draconians had said. They were looking for a treasure at Mountainhome. Tatelyn knew of the town. It was much like Forestedge, a small, obscure village set higher in the Vingaard Mountains. If there was a treasure there, Tatelyn had certainly never heard tell of it. But the draconians were convinced that something was at the village, something valuable.

Simle's pace slowed as the sun came up, then stopped

entirely. They'd been running half the night. Reluctantly, Tatelyn opened her eyes. They were on a thin dirt path that cut up the mountainside between thick trees. Tatelyn could see a few houses ahead on either side of the path. They were built closer together as the path wound upward.

"Who goes there?" A voice rang out in the still morning air. "Don't move."

Tatelyn and Simle both looked around. Simle soon focused on something Tatelyn could not see. The dragon must have keener senses than she did. Tatelyn didn't see anything but a tall stand of trees, but she addressed the voice in that direction.

"I am Tatelyn of Forestedge. My companion is a bronze dragon. We've come to warn your village."

"Warn us? Of what?" The voice now seemed more concerned.

Simle turned her head. "There are four of them," she murmured to Tatelyn.

"Where? I can't see them!" Tatelyn scanned the trees and rocks in frustration.

"Just trust me," Simle said. "Now explain to the guard before we get shot!"

Tatelyn glared at Simle, then turned back to where she thought the guard was. "I was captured by draconians about half a day's journey to the north. This dragon fought them, but at least three escaped and there may be others. They plan to attack your village and steal your treasure."

The trees and rocks seemed to come alive. Four people, all armed with bows and dressed in green and gray to blend with the foliage, strode from their hiding places. While three of them kept their bows trained on Tatelyn, the fourth, a young man perhaps a year or two older than Tatelyn with freckled skin, walked toward them with his weapon lowered. Tufts of red hair stuck out from underneath his leather cap. As he walked toward them he took off the cap and shook out his shockingly bright red curls.

"No wonder he wears that cap," Simle whispered to Tatelyn. "Even you could have spotted him without it."

Tatelyn stifled a grin and shushed the dragon. The boy was getting close enough to hear them.

"I am Molot Auricwatch, one of the guards of Mountainhome. Did you say draconians are planning to come here?"

Tatelyn nodded. "They seek a treasure here. They . . ." Tatelyn found herself growing weak and limp. Breathing heavily, she leaned against Simle.

"Do you have a healer here?" Simle asked. "A cleric? My . . . companion is hurt, as am I. I do not know if you will treat a dragon, but . . ."

"Of course we will treat a dragon," Molot said, bowing deeply to Simle. Tatelyn and Simle both started. "You are most welcome here, benevolent bronze creature. May we have the honor of knowing your name?"

"Uh . . ." Simle looked as completely taken aback as Tatelyn was. Not even in Palanthas had Tatelyn ever seen such an attitude toward dragons. This boy regarded Simle as though she were royalty. The other three had the same respectful, almost reverent manner.

"I am Simle," the dragon said after a long moment.

"Welcome to Mountainhome, Simle," said one of the other guards. "We shall escort you and your friend to our village, where you may rest as long as you like."

"We're not—" both Tatelyn and Simle began, but their protests were lost as the four humans bustled about them. They lifted Tatelyn onto a makeshift stretcher formed by a blanket and two branches and began to carry her up the path. Molot beckoned for Simle to follow.

"Do you have strength enough to talk?" Molot asked Tatelyn. "Your injuries appear grave, yet you seem more alert than many people I've seen with lesser wounds."

Tatelyn looked at Simle. An unspoken question passed between them. Simle blinked slowly, and Tatelyn sighed. She supposed they couldn't treat her or the dragon adequately without knowing the details of their plight. "The dragon and I are under a spell. What happens to her, I feel. What happens to me, she feels."

Molot looked from dragon to girl then dragon again.

"The dragon feels your pain? And you feel hers?"

"Yes. We were traveling to Palanthas to find more about this spell and how to undo it. Then the draconians found me."

"More on this spell later," said the man pulling the travois. "Tell us all you heard from the draconians."

Tatelyn told them what she remembered, which was not much. Still, it seemed to be enough for the men, who began discussing defense of the village. They stopped at a small, neat cottage just off the trail.

"Tatelyn, this is my family's house," Molot said. "While we have no cleric, you will find my mother is an excellent healer." He turned to Simle. "We have a villager who knows something of dragon medicine. He shall tend to you. We can also offer you some of our finest livestock. I know it isn't what you're used to, but we get few fish up here."

Tatelyn's mouth dropped open. These people were giving Simle their animals? Simle considered this offer for the time it took to blink one bronze eyelid, then followed one of the men up the mountain, where the land leveled out into a field dotted with cattle.

The men pulled Tatelyn to the cottage door and knocked. The door swung open, revealing a thin, older woman with bright red hair tied into a rough bun. Her freckled hands flew to her mouth when she saw Tatelyn's injuries.

"Mother, this is Tatelyn. She came here with a bronze dragon." Molot nodded to the two men, who let the travois down gently, then walked back in the direction they had just come, probably to resume their guard posts.

"A bronze dragon? You are a lucky girl indeed."

"I've had nothing but bad luck since that dragon came into my life," Tatelyn said.

"Nonsense," the woman retorted. "Dragons such as that make the best companions. Let's get you to where old Yanna can tend to you." Yanna and Molot lifted Tatelyn as though she weighed no more than a house cat and carried her to a cot by the fire.

"Molot, go help the others tend to that dragon," Yanna said, examining Tatelyn's wounds. "I can handle the girl." Molot nodded to Tatelyn and left the cottage, gathering a few herbs on his way out the door. Yanna pulled a bit of Tatelyn's robe out of a dried wound, bracing herself for a scream or at least a wince, but none came.

"Child, what is the matter? Didn't that hurt?" She poked the burn around Tatelyn's wrist.

Tatelyn shook her head. As Yanna washed her wounds carefully with warm water that smelled strongly of raspberries, Tatelyn told her all that had befallen her.

"The dragon saw this pendant"—Tatelyn showed the necklace to Yanna, who flashed a quick glance at it and returned to her work—"and assumed that I had something to do with her mother because her mother gave her an identical one. When I fitted the pieces together, our pain was swapped. What happens to me, she feels, and I feel hers—and both of our magic has stopped working. We were trying to go to Palanthas to ask Elistan about the necklace."

Yanna stopped cleaning one of Tatelyn's wounds and peered at her. "We know Elistan's name, even here. You wear the robes of a cleric. Do you heal dragons?"

The question was so absurd that Tatelyn burst into laughter. "Hardly! I would rather every dragon be banished from Krynn."

Yanna was now stirring a paste in a bowl and applying it to some fresh cloths. From the smell, it was the same flowers Tatelyn had used earlier to treat herself and Simle. Was that the evening before? It seemed like an eternity.

"Are you one of the Heirs of Huma?" Yanna asked. "We've seen your kind before."

"I am. My friends and I travel about Solamnia, seeking other people who would like the dragons to leave."

"Why on Krynn would you want the dragons to leave?" Yanna said. "This village wouldn't be standing were it not for the actions of a gold dragon." Yanna looked out the window at the town. "We were occupied during the war. Draconians and goblins used this town for barracks. We were forced to work for them, slaving day and night. Then Fari, a gold dragon, came and liberated us."

Yanna finished tying a bandage around Tatelyn's burned wrist with a flourish. "You do the dragons a great disservice by trying to get them to leave. They deserve a place in this world, even the evil ones."

"We got along just fine for thousands of years without the dragons. The Heirs of Huma only wish that they return to their homeland."

Yanna sniffed. "One of your followers from Forestedge came here seeking members. He was laughed out of the town gates. You might want to keep a low profile here. No recruiting."

"Don't worry," Tatelyn muttered. "As soon as Simle and I heal, we'll be on our way."

Yanna softened. "Don't rush off. You've done us a great service, letting us know of the draconians. I just think you should reconsider your mission." Yanna went to the table and looked at the herb jars Molot had opened. She shook her head. "He forgot the garlic. Will you be all right by yourself for a moment? I'll come back and make you some soup."

"I'll be fine." Tatelyn lay back on the simple, but comfortable, cot.

"I won't be long." Yanna walked to the door, then turned back. "Even Huma loved a silver dragon."

Tatelyn's head whipped toward Yanna. "What did you say?" But the woman had left, swinging the door shut behind her.

CHAPTER TWELVE

The people of Mountainhome kept bringing Simle all manner of creatures until she had eaten her fill. Although it was strange and heavier than the fish and plants she was used to, she soon began to enjoy the new meats. She now knew the names of the delicious animals humans kept for food: cow, pig, goat, sheep, chicken. The chicken was particularly good, once she figured out how to keep the feathers out of her teeth.

As soon as they were assured that Simle had eaten her fill, the humans all left to prepare Mountainhome's defenses, save one old man, easily the oldest human she had seen yet. He walked slightly stooped and had no hair at all atop his head. A long beard trailed from his chin, making his head look as though it was put on upside down. Simle giggled and the man looked at her with deep brown, almost black, eyes.

"Do you find me amusing, youngster?" the man asked, pointing his gnarled wooden cane at Simle. Simle looked behind her, certain the man was addressing someone else.

"No, I meant you, Bronzeling." The man walked closer, smiling.

Simle drew herself to her full height and looked down at him. "I must be twice your age!"

"Easy," the man said, motioning for Simle to sit down. Simle remained standing. "I think we are close in age by years, but you are much younger in measure of wisdom—younger than old Aggy."

Simle snorted, making Aggy's beard ripple. "What wisdom can a human have?"

"Well," Aggy said, pulling out a rolled piece of leather and unfurling it on the ground. It held small wooden tools, bandages, and little vials of liquids and pastes. "I do have the wisdom needed to heal an injured dragon."

"An injured bronze dragon?" Simle asked.

"Most of my experience is with Gold, but yes, I can treat a Bronze." Aggy held up one vial, uncorked it, and held it under Simle's nose. Her eyes widened at the smell.

"That's the kelp my mother uses on shark bites!"

Aggy nodded. "Bring your head down here, little one," he said. Simle doubted this man would have a touch as gentle as her mother's, but she complied anyway, suddenly missing her mother.

Aggy dipped a flat wooden stick into the vial and

began applying it to the worst of Simle's wounds.

"It doesn't sting?" Aggy observed.

"No," Simle said. "Somewhere in your village there's a human girl yelping in pain."

Aggy patted the last of the salve onto Simle's wounds. "I heard. What wizardry did that to a dragon and a girl? And why?"

"I wish I knew," Simle said. "You never heard of such a thing?"

Aggy shook his head. "Never."

"Have you heard of draconians?"

"Of course," Aggy said. "Who hasn't?"

As much as Simle hated to admit ignorance of anything humans considered common knowledge, she had to know. "I haven't. What can you tell me of them?"

"They're new to Krynn," Aggy said as he examined the marks the blast had left on Simle's face. "Fierce fighters, loyal to Takhisis. They were created from the eggs of the good dragons. That's why—"

Simle stood up quickly, knocking Aggy to the ground. "What did you just say? About the eggs?"

"Draconians are created by corrupting the eggs of good dragons, using the darkest, most horrible magic," Aggy said, watching Simle closely. "You didn't know this?"

Simle could not respond, trembling with horror and rage. This, then, was the fate of her siblings.

Not imprisoned or killed, as she often imagined, but transformed into beasts that served the evil goddess. Transformed into the creatures she had fought. Why had her parents not told her this? Slumping, Simle wondered if it would have made any difference.

"The draconians I fought exploded when killed. Do you know which eggs made them?" Simle whispered.

Aggy's eyes held pity. "Those are bozac draconians. They're formed from bronze dragon eggs." He finished treating the last wound on Simle's face and patted her shoulder gently. "I am sorry, Bronzeling."

Simle jerked away from Aggy. "Who are you to feel sorry for me? Your kind made those draconians! You stole my siblings before they were even born!" Simle stalked off, pausing once to breathe back at Aggy. Of course, her breath weapons were gone, so all she got for her trouble was making his beard wave in the wind again.

Simle stumbled to the edge of the village. One of the guards who had earlier escorted her and Tatelyn waved. "Don't wander far!" he called to her with a smile. "We'll need your help later."

Simle said nothing, but glared at the man so fiercely that he blanched and returned to reinforcing the village wall. These humans expected her to fight for them? Against creatures who were her kin? Those draconians could have been her brothers and sisters!

Simle couldn't leave Tatelyn, no matter how much she wanted to. But she had to get away from these humans. She scanned the edges of the village. To the east, a wide stream trickled down from the mountain. It didn't look very deep, but it would have to do.

Simle raced to the water and flung herself into it with a splash. The rocks underneath scraped her belly, but she didn't care. Hearing the waves was like hearing her mother's voice again. That thought saddened her even more. Was Mother all right? Simle should never have left home.

A twig snapped behind her. Simle rose out of the water and whirled around. Were the draconians here so soon? Relatives or not, they had established themselves to be enemies. But even with her sharp senses, she couldn't detect a threat. Still, perhaps she should find cover.

Simle looked for a place to hide. The only thing that might even begin to conceal her was a large outcropping of rock. She ducked behind it and tucked in her head and tail. She wished she had her magic back so she could turn into a squirrel, or a fish, or a bird. If they weren't looking closely, she might be able to surprise them.

Simle could hear voices now, but no words. It didn't sound like the draconians. More humans. Simle rose from behind the rock and peered over. There were two of them, a boy and a girl. The girl screamed, which quickly told

Simle these humans weren't from Mountainhome. Simle leaped toward them, thankful her reflexes weren't as slow as a human's. The two started to duck back into the forest, but soon Simle had them both cornered against the rock.

Up close, Simle realized that what she took for two humans cowering before her were actually a human girl with golden curls coiled tightly against her head and a dusky-skinned half-elf boy, who both looked about Tatelyn's age. And both of them looked familiar.

"I know you," she said, pacing before them. "You tried to capture me."

The boy drew his bow. Simle knocked it out of his hand as easily as she might have swatted a minnow. Unfazed, he drew a short sword and pointed it at her.

"You killed Tatelyn. For that I will fight you, even if it means my death."

Simle laughed, infuriating the boy even more. The girl, however, remained pale and silent. Simle recognized her from before—this was the wizard who had attacked her. Judging from the rich fabric of her clothes and the jewels at her throat, Simle could tell she was wealthy. Despite her riches and whatever magic she'd possessed the other day, the girl was now struck motionless with fear.

The half-elf turned a brilliant scarlet. "How dare you laugh about killing her!" he snapped.

Simle tried to speak but couldn't, her sides heaving with laugher. If it weren't for the fact that she had the two humans cornered, they could have walked off. She wouldn't have stopped them. The hilarity of the situation soon faded, however, and Simle sputtered, "I didn't kill Tatelyn! Killing her would only hurt me!"

"Start making sense," the wizard said finally. "Where is Tatelyn?"

As much as Simle feared Tatelyn getting back with her dragon-hunting friends, perhaps these two would be of some help. Wizards in particular were known for being clever, even among dragons. The quicker she and Tatelyn figured out how to undo this magic, the sooner she could leave this world of humans and return home. "I will take you to Tatelyn, but not because you're pointing that sword at me. Lower it."

The boy did not move.

"I am warning you, human," Simle said. "The village where Tatelyn stays reveres my kind and is preparing for battle. If you walk into the village with that pointed at me, you'll be overcome swiftly, and not by me."

The half-elf slowly sheathed his sword.

"That's better. Follow me." Simle led the two humans to the cottage where Tatelyn rested. Along the way, the villagers smiled at Simle and looked curiously at the two humans following her.

Simle heard the girl whisper to the boy, "The dragon's right. These people do seem to revere her."

"More misguided souls," the boy said. "Tatelyn will know best how to convert them to our cause."

"She hasn't had much success so far," Simle said. The boy and girl both jumped. "For all the time you spend crusading against dragons, you never once learned we have excellent hearing?" Simle sniped.

The girl, at least, had the grace to look ashamed as they reached the door of the cottage. "Your friend is in there," Simle said. Neither human moved. The girl stared at the ground and clutched her small bag tightly to her chest.

Humans! Simle rolled her eyes and knocked on the door with one claw.

CHAPTER THIRTEEN

Tatelyn drifted on a wave of near sleep brought on by the herbs Yanna had given her. She walked among the stars in the sky, between a large figure eight and a platinum dragon. Why did Paladine adopt the form of a dragon? The dragons could be corrupted—Paladine should know that better than anyone.

The constellation of the Platinum Dragon moved across the sky. It walked to the figure eight and twined itself about it. Then the Platinum Dragon tucked his tail under his chin, so he formed a figure eight with his own body. His head turned toward Tatelyn, and even though there were no stars to form his eyes, Tatelyn knew she was being watched.

"Why do you fight us?"

Tatelyn could not see the mouth that formed the words, but she knew they came from the dragon—from Paladine.

"I do not fight you, my lord," she said. "I only wish

you to remove the dragons from this world, like they were before."

"The dragons are my children, as are you. They come and go as they are needed," the Platinum Dragon said.

"We don't need them anymore. Can the Whitestone Council convince them to return home?" The Platinum Dragon laughed with a sound like church bells and rushing water. "You seek to convince a dragon to do anything? You have much to learn—too much for you to separate from your dragon companion now."

"She is not my companion!" Tatelyn shouted.

"My dear, are you all right?" Yanna rushed to Tatelyn's cot. Tatelyn lay in the cottage, with her wounds treated and still not hurting.

Tatelyn tried to remember the fleeting images of the dream, but all she could recall was the image of a dragon coiled into a figure eight. "I'm fine. Only a dream."

Yanna opened her mouth as if to say more, but a loud knock on the door echoed through the cottage.

"Who can that be? Everyone knows not to bother me when I have a patient." Yanna hurried to the door. Simle's large bronze form stood outside, blocking the midday light.

"Ah, you must be Tatelyn's companion," Yanna said.

"She isn't my companion!" Simle and Tatelyn both said. Yanna laughed.

"Whether the two of you like it or not, you are companions," Yanna said. "Some power higher than the both of you has determined that."

"I won't speak of this with yet another human." Simle rolled her eyes, which made her huge head bump the doorjamb. Tatelyn yelped.

"That's not why I knocked," Simle said. "There are some people here to see Tatelyn."

Tatelyn sat straight up in bed. Was this a trick? But no, there were Elrit and Ramma behind Simle. What a relief to see familiar faces!

"Move, you great beast," Tatelyn said. "Let them in."

"A simple thank you would have been nice," Simle grumbled, but she stood aside to let Elrit and Ramma enter the cottage. The two of them raced to Tatelyn's side and embraced her.

"Now, now," Yanna said, pulling them away from Tatelyn. "Even if she feels no pain, crushing her will not aid her healing. Sit down and talk to her like civilized beings." She pulled up two light cane chairs and pointed to them. Elrit and Ramma sat down meekly.

"As for you"—Yanna turned to Simle, still standing in the door—"there's no room for you in here and I need my door. If you'd like to join the conversation, there is a window right there."

"Oh, no!" Tatelyn began, but Simle interrupted her.

"Thank you, I think I will!" She disappeared from the door, and moments later her face reappeared in the window.

"Forget it," Tatelyn said. "Elrit, close the shutters!"

Elrit moved toward the window, but Simle growled and he stepped back. "Why can't I listen?" Simle pouted.

Tatelyn sighed. Given the dragon's sharp hearing, eavesdropping would be ridiculously easy. "Will you be quiet while we talk, at least?" Tatelyn asked.

"Perhaps." Simle grinned.

"Please?" Tatelyn asked. She groaned and turned to Elrit and Ramma. After spending so much time among strange faces, they were a most welcome sight. Tatelyn explained what had happened. Simle filled in some details, but Elrit and Ramma were silent until they had finished their tale.

"I have never heard of such a thing," Ramma said. "Never in all the stories."

"Me neither," Elrit said. "I've heard of similarly strange things from seafaring folk, but nothing like this. You have no idea how you can break this spell?"

"None at all," Tatelyn said, leaning back on the cot. "We hoped that Elistan might be able to help us, but we ended up here."

"A shame one of the clerics didn't come with us," Ramma said. "They could have healed you."

"How did you find me? We didn't leave a trail, at least not until we got off the mountain."

"Well," Ramma began, fiddling with one of her spell pouches. "We wanted to find you, but . . ." She stared at the floor.

"Rogan said it was a waste of time," Elrit finished. "He said the dragon would have killed you and we best continue to the Whitestone Council."

Tatelyn gaped. Rogan was fanatically dedicated to the Heirs of Huma, but to coldheartedly abandon her—

"Your parents were very upset," Ramma said quickly, seeing the look on Tatelyn's face. "Elrit and I promised we'd find you. I used my magic and he used his tracking skills to pick up your trail."

"It was easy once Simle wasn't able to fly." Elrit looked up at Simle, amused. "It doesn't take much skill to spot where a dragon landed in a field!" Simle reached through the window and thumped him on the head with one claw.

"Simle, stop that!" Tatelyn said, then turned to Elrit. "Thank you," Tatelyn said. "I'm very grateful."

"The others headed to the council," Ramma said. "We hoped to meet them once we found you."

Tatelyn nodded thoughtfully, wondering how long it would take to get to Palanthas to have the spell removed. Could she make it back to the council in time? It seemed impossible. One thing about Elrit and Ramma finding her suddenly struck her. "Ramma," she said, "I don't know how to say this . . ." She trailed off, uncertain how to ask without offending. "I mean, don't think I'm not grateful, but you've never been the . . . outdoorsy type. You've never even left the caravan before, wouldn't even go hunting. Why did you come?"

A blush traveled up Ramma's neck and spread over her face. "Rogan is starting to frighten me," Ramma said. "He was different when we first met you, Tatelyn, but now he's obsessed with banishing the dragons. I fear he's no longer in his right mind, especially now. In your absence, the Heirs of Huma looked to him for guidance. I fear that he'll try to wage war on the dragons, not petition them to leave."

"No one can win that war," Elrit said. "We barely survived a war with the chromatic dragons. We need you back, Tatelyn."

Tatelyn sighed. She wasn't altogether surprised to hear about Rogan. He was a strong leader, but he also was prone to raving, and Ramma wasn't the only one who had been worried. And Elrit was right—a war could never end well.

Ramma fiddled with a bag she carried. Tatelyn thought she was merely fidgeting, but then Ramma drew forth a battered volume from the bag.

"Ever since I saw the pendant you wear, Tatelyn, I couldn't shake the feeling that I'd seen it before. I began to look through the books I brought from home."

"You brought books?" Elrit exclaimed. "We told you to travel lightly!"

Ramma glared at him. "These books contain a lot of lore about dragons. I thought they might be of some use."

"Rightly so," Tatelyn said. "Elrit, it isn't like she brought her full wardrobe with her!"

"Have you looked in your wagon?" Elrit asked.

"Quiet!" Simle roared. "What is with mortals and your petty bickering? Allow the girl to continue!"

Ramma flipped through the book until she reached a page marked with a long satin ribbon. Holding it up so they all could see, Ramma pointed to a sketch: a whole piece of jewelry that was definitely formed by the two pieces Tatelyn and Simle bore. Both Tatelyn and Simle bent closer to the page with a gasp.

"I knew I had seen this before," said Ramma. "I searched through all my books and found it in this book about Huma."

"Huma!" Tatelyn said. "Elistan said this jewel belonged to Huma. But how would Simle's mother get the other half?"

"My mother gave it to me, but I don't know where it came from." Simle's eyes clouded and she stared at the picture. Tatelyn hoped she wouldn't cry, for any tears would splash down on the bed where Tatelyn was lying.

"Tatelyn, you know the story of the Silver Dragon?"

"Of course. People insist on telling it to me to show that dragons can do some good in the world."

"I don't know the story," Simle said. "Which silver dragon?"

"The book doesn't give a name," Ramma continued. "However, she took human form and met a knight named Huma. They fell in love and could have lived together in this world happily."

"Happily with a human!" Simle snorted. "Silver dragons always were a bit strange."

Ramma ignored Simle. "At the same time, Takhisis was trying to take over the world. Huma was offered a choice: He and the silver dragon could remain in this world and live their lives, but the evil dragons would remain. Or he could be given the dragonlance and he and his love could fight Takhisis and drive her and the evil dragons from this world forever."

"He chose to fight Takhisis and drive the dragons from this world," Tatelyn said. "He kept Krynn for the mortals, not the dragons. Once the evil dragons were banished, the good dragons left to keep the balance. That's why we call ourselves the Heirs of Huma."

"You named your group after a man who loved a dragon?" Simle said. "I knew humans didn't always think clearly, but—"

"That's not the point!" Ramma snapped. Elrit and Tatelyn stared at her. "I found something about this jewel. It's a Starjewel, often exchanged by elf lovers forced to part. It forges a link between their souls, allowing them to share each other's emotions even when half a world a way."

"Lovers!" Tatelyn and Simle both looked like they had eaten lemons. Elrit snickered.

Ramma shook the book at them. "Don't you see? I think you're wearing a piece of the Starjewel that the silver dragon gave Huma."

Everyone gaped at Ramma. Tatelyn found her voice first. "That's absurd!"

"Is it?" Ramma said. "Elistan himself told you your jewel once belonged to Huma. It would explain what happened to you both. Really, what do you think would happen if two beings with no prior connection, who hated each other just because of what they were, wore two halves of the same Starjewel?"

Simle blinked very slowly. "This makes sense. But how do we undo this switch, now that we know how it occurred?"

"That I can't say," Ramma said, closing the book with

a soft thump. "I've been through the books twice and can't find anything about a spell like yours."

"As soon as Tatelyn can travel, we'll continue to Palanthas," Simle said.

"We'll come with you," Elrit said.

"I don't want more mortals tagging along with me!" Simle glowered at Elrit, but Elrit no longer seemed as cowed by her.

"They will come with us," Tatelyn said. "What if I'm hurt again? You can't heal me and you can't bind a wound with your claws."

"Fine, then. Let's bring the whole village with us!" Simle turned from the window and stomped off.

Tatelyn flopped back against the pillows. "I can't wait to be rid of that beast."

Chapter Fourteen

Simle had not stalked very far from the cottage when she heard a voice behind her. Turning, she saw Ramma.

"What do you want?" she growled, not stopping. The wizard followed her as she strode out of the village.

"I want to ask you some questions about that pendant you wear," Ramma said, panting to keep up with the dragon's stride. "You said your mother gave it to you?"

"Yes," Simle said through gritted teeth. The pendant thumped against her chest with each step, seeming to mock her.

"Do you have any idea where she got it?" Ramma tripped over her skirts as they passed through the village gates. Simle heard one of the guards snicker, but Ramma either didn't hear or chose to ignore him.

"What does it matter?" Simle turned left into a rocky area between the forest and town. Perhaps the girl wouldn't follow her through the rough landscape. But a clatter behind Simle told her that Ramma was still following her. This human was persistent.

"We need to know as much as we can about that pendant," Ramma pointed out. She took her skirts in both hands so she wouldn't trip. "Even once we get to Palanthas, Elistan can only tell us about Tatelyn's half. We have to figure out where yours came from."

Simle sighed deeply. "My mother was protecting humans. A . . ." What was the word her father had used? "A pilgrimage."

Ramma's green eyes brightened. "A pilgrimage? To where?"

"I don't know!" Simle whirled to face the girl. Ramma took a step back and nearly lost her balance. "I don't know why my parents had to protect humans! What good are they?"

Before Ramma could reply, shouting reached their ears. "Draconians! Draconians!" The cry echoed from the town up to the rocky hillside.

"We should go back." Ramma's freckles stood out against her pale skin. As she turned back to the village, a draconian rounded the corner of the cottage and tackled her. Ramma beat at the draconian with her fist, but it held her to the ground firmly with one hand. With its other hand, it held a sword at her throat.

Simle roared and rushed toward the draconian. It turned to her, its eyes widening. Simle knocked the draconian off Ramma and broke its neck with one strong blow.

"Run!" she cried to Ramma. She and the girl raced from the draconian before it exploded, flinging dirt and bits of bone everywhere.

"What happened?" Ramma asked Simle as they ran to the rocks at the edge of the village.

"They explode when they're killed," Simle said. "Stay here. Maybe you can use your magic from above." Ramma huddled in a hidden nook of rock, watching Simle race to the village path. Draconians swarmed all over the hill leading to the village. Some of them even flew short distances through the air, hurling fire down at the gates. The villagers were ready with water, however, and put out the fires as quickly as they started. The draconians had not breached the gate yet. The villagers kept them at bay with arrows and spears. Simle smiled. The draconians must not have been expecting to find the village ready for them.

"You!" roared a voice behind Simle. She spun about to find the leader of the draconians who had captured Tatelyn. He walked toward her, sword dripping with red blood. Human blood. Simle found herself angered at the sight, and wondered why.

"You are far too meddlesome, even for a metallic dragon. Why fight for these creatures?" The draconian gestured about the village. "They are nothing to beings such as us. Many of your kin have fought for them with no hope of reward or even thanks. Leave them to us and we won't hinder your leaving."

Simle looked carefully at the draconian's face, seeking some hint of relation. Could they really be formed from bronze dragon eggs?

"We could have been siblings," the draconian said, echoing Simle's own thoughts. "Go. This fight is not your fight."

Simle found herself agreeing with this draconian. She could find Tatelyn and fly away with her, then leave her when they got their curse lifted. They were almost completely healed—they had no need of these humans. She turned back to the rocks where Ramma hid. Her gaze locked with Ramma's, who crouched behind the rocks. The girl's eyes were filled with fear verging on panic.

"What are you looking at?" the draconian said. It followed Simle's gaze, spotted the human, and grinned. "Ah. Stand aside, Bronzeling." The draconian raised his sword, shouting a guttural battle cry as he advanced toward the girl.

Simle leaped in front of him, snarling. The draconian laughed. "So, you have chosen a side. It will do her no good." He gestured behind Simle and she turned to see two other draconians flanking her. Both had arrows pointed at Simle's wings.

"Stop me and you may never fly again," the leader said. "This human is nothing to you. Leave and we won't follow or harm you."

Simle froze. She couldn't fly now, but to think she might never fly again chilled her heart. She glanced from side to side. The draconians were well positioned. If she took one of the archers out, the other would still have a good shot at her wings. The leader nodded to Simle mockingly and took another step toward Ramma.

With a cry, Simle sprang forward onto the leader. He only had time to utter a surprised grunt before she slit his throat with one sharp claw. She picked him up and flung him toward one of the archers. "Ramma, duck!" she yelled. The archer started to duck, but the leader's body exploded right on top of him. Simle whipped around to see the other archer running toward her. Simle thrust her tail out to trip the draconian, but it jumped nimbly over it and brought its sword down on Simle's back. It missed her wings, but the blow shook Simle's body.

The draconian raised the sword for another blow. Simle managed to slide away and the sword plunged harmlessly into the grass. Before the draconian could yank it free, Simle gave two swipes of her claws. The draconian fell to the ground. Simle ran to the crevice where Ramma hid, stretching her body to cover the opening. The force of the explosion nearly knocked Simle into Ramma, but she kept the worst of blast from the girl. Once it was over, Simle rolled over to the side as Ramma slowly emerged from the crevice. She leaned against the rocks, breathing heavily. "You saved me. You risked your wings to save me."

"I . . ." Simle tried to remember. Why had she done it? Simle tried to recall the fight, some reason for protecting this human. "I don't know," she finally said.

Ramma stared at the dragon. After a moment, she began walking back to the village, but Simle heard her whisper as she walked away.

"Thank you."

CHAPTER FIFTEEN

After Ramma left the cottage, Elrit and Tatelyn sat for a while in silence. Tatelyn was glad that Elrit had come after her, especially since Rogan was so prepared to leave her for dead.

As if reading her thoughts, Elrit said, "I hope Rogan isn't mad at me."

"For coming after me?"

"No. He might think Ramma and I eloped."

Tatelyn began to giggle. It had been a long time since she'd laughed, truly laughed, and it felt good.

"It is nice to hear you laugh, child," Yanna said, bringing two bowls of soup. Elrit dived into his, while Tatelyn played with the spoon.

"Aren't you hungry?" Elrit said, looking up from his half-finished bowl.

"I might be," Tatelyn said. "I haven't really eaten since yesterday. But only Simle would know."

"I've been thinking," Yanna said, sitting down with

her own bowl of soup. "There may be something nearby that could help you and Simle. Mountainhome keeps many secret treasures. That's why the draconians were coming, from what you said. One of those secrets is a pool hidden deep in the mountains. It holds much knowledge, and if you choose to go there you may find out more about this pendant you wear."

"Perhaps how to break the spell?" Tatelyn could hardly breathe.

"Perhaps." Yanna took Tatelyn's bowl of untouched soup. "Perhaps not. The pool can be choosy about to whom it will reveal its secrets."

"Tatelyn, we have to go there!" Elrit rose to his feet, but before he could move farther, there was a loud explosion and the ground shook beneath them. Earthenware jars leaped off the shelves and crashed to the floor, spilling herbs.

"Over here!" Yanna shouted. Elrit pulled Tatelyn out of bed and half carried, half dragged her to the front doorway. The three of them braced themselves in the frame until the shaking stopped.

"What was that?" Elrit asked, peering out the door.

"The draconians," Tatelyn said, remembering the fight Simle had before. "They explode when killed."

Yanna gasped. "How horrible!" She began gathering up herbs and putting them in a basket she tied at her waist. "I'll go see if anyone needs help."

"Now?" Tatelyn said. "You're crazy! They could still be out there!"

"That's why they'll need my help." She grabbed a fistful of dried leaves from one of the broken jars on the floor, then fastened the lid on the basket.

"I'll go with you," Elrit said. He rose to his feet, but Yanna pushed him back down.

"No, you stay here with Tatelyn. She encountered these beasts before and escaped. Who knows what they'd do to her if they find her?" With those comforting words, Yanna raced out the door, leaving herb dust in her wake.

Elrit placed a hand on Tatelyn's undamaged shoulder. "What did they do to you?"

Tatelyn shuddered. "I'd rather not talk about it now."

"The dragon saved you, didn't she?" Elrit glanced out the open door. "It seems as though everything I ever thought about dragons was turned upside down today. First I see how these villagers revere a bronze dragon, then I find that the founder of the Heirs of Huma herself has been saved by a dragon."

"Well, I doubt she would've saved me if we weren't linked," Tatelyn said. "Saving me meant she wouldn't feel my pain."

"Still," Elrit said. "I see how they treat Simle, and

how they treat you. As if you're equals and friends. Is it possible that people like these, who took you in and healed you, would love an evil creature?" Elrit's green eyes searched Tatelyn's violet ones.

Tatelyn opened her mouth to answer, but a horrible yell made her and Elrit look up. A draconian raced toward them, sword raised. Elrit pushed Tatelyn back inside the house and drew his bow, loosing an arrow that bounced harmlessly off the draconian's armor. Elrit flung his bow to the side and drew his sword as the draconian reached the cottage.

Tatelyn shrank back in the cottage as swords struck each other again and again. Her hands shook and she realized that she still felt the ill effects of fear, even though she no longer felt pain. This was the same type of draconian that had tortured her in the forest.

Elrit faltered and the draconian struck him across one arm. He switched his sword to his other hand, but he wasn't as adept with that arm. Tatelyn had to do something. But what could she do without her clerical powers?

Looking wildly around the cottage for something, anything that could be a weapon, Tatelyn spotted a poker near the hearth. Praying to Mishakal that her legs would not collapse, she ran across the room and grabbed the poker with her good arm. Elrit and the draconian were still fighting, but Elrit's blows were becoming more erratic.

With a loud cry, Tatelyn ran back to the doorway. Shoving Elrit out of the way, she thrust the poker into the draconian's throat. It stumbled back two paces, then collapsed just outside the front door.

"Tatelyn, move!" Elrit grabbed Tatelyn and half carried, half flung her across the room. Moments later, the draconian exploded, sending chunks of wood and dried mud flying everywhere. When the debris cleared, Tatelyn looked back at the door—or, what used to be the door. A large, jagged hole now provided entrance to Yanna's cottage.

Elrit shook his head. "I didn't know you could fight," he said, getting to his feet and offering a hand to Tatelyn.

"Neither did I," Tatelyn said, allowing Elrit to pull her off the floor with his good arm. She sat back down on the bed before she unwittingly did any damage to herself. "Draconians terrify me. I just had no choice."

"I'm glad you did," Elrit said. "I think he would have gotten the better of me in the end. It would be only fitting, I suppose." Elrit then clamped his mouth shut as though he had said too much.

"Why would that be fitting?"

"I told you a silver dragon killed my parents."

Tatelyn nodded. That was the story Elrit told when they spoke at various towns.

"I never told you that I know why the dragon killed them. My parents were carrying cargo on that last voyage—silver dragon eggs."

"Silver dragon eggs," Tatelyn murmured, not quite understanding. "But if they carried eggs, then why would a silver dragon . . ."

"They were to become draconians!" Elrit burst out. "My parents were transporting eggs so that they could be transformed into those beasts! My parents didn't care. All my parents heard was the sound of steel being dropped into their palms."

Tatelyn gasped, startled at the mercenary bent of Elrit's parents. "Then the dragon—"

"Was only trying to protect her eggs from a fate worse than death. That night I heard my parents shouting orders and I ran up on deck. I looked up at the sky and saw a huge shape blotting out the stars—a dragon. The moonlight reflected off its scales and I could see it was a silver dragon. I had never seen a dragon, but I always thought the silver ones were good. And then . . ." Elrit choked.

Tatelyn reached out and patted his shoulder. "It's all right," she said. "I know what happened."

"No, you don't!" Elrit burst out. "That silver dragon

must have been trying to rescue them. She kept diving at us, but not attacking. She must have seen that she couldn't save the eggs, so she sank the ship." Elrit's eyes glittered fiercely. "She killed her own eggs, rather than let them turn into draconians."

Tatelyn shuddered. She had heard tales of people killing their children rather than letting them be taken by the enemy. Were dragons so different from humans? Tatelyn struggled for something to say and could think of nothing. Suddenly, her grief over Brigg seemed so small. She at least had known him very well, probably better than she knew herself. To have lost your parents and still, years after the fact, have to question what you knew about them seemed such a heavy burden. She would do anything if she could only tell Elrit that his parents were certainly good people caught in a situation they didn't understand. She would even spend the rest of her life linked to Simle if she could only take away Elrit's pain.

Ramma appeared in the doorway, breathing heavily and covered with dust and scratches. She looked satisfied despite her disarray.

"Are you all right?" Tatelyn asked. "The battle?"

"The villagers have it under control. With Simle's help. I blasted a couple draconians with magic myself on my way here." Ramma rushed forward, looking at the damaged cottage. "Are you all right? Elrit, your arm!"

Tatelyn and Ramma used Yanna's supplies to bind Elrit's wound. As they did, Tatelyn told Ramma about the pool.

"As soon as Simle gets back," Tatelyn said, "we'll go there."

CHAPTER SIXTEEN

When Ramma left Simle after thanking her, Simle hurried into the village. The damage there wasn't nearly as bad as she thought it would be. The draconians were fierce, but these humans, kind as they were to Simle, appeared to be staunch fighters when their homes were threatened. There was damage to the outer walls where some of the draconians had exploded, but they never breached the village proper, past the first few cottages outside the walls. A sigh escaped Simle's nostrils, then she blinked, surprised. Why should she feel relief? Humans were nothing to her, after all.

"Simle!"

The dragon turned to see Molot striding toward her. "They're gone! We have either killed or chased away all of them. A few villagers fell during the battle," Molot said, bowing his head. "But only a small fraction of what we would have lost had you and Tatelyn not warned us. And had you not helped us fight."

"I did no more than repay my debt to you," she said, running one claw through the dirt.

Molot raised an eyebrow. "Is that the only reason you helped?"

Simle prepared to refute him, but the human changed the subject. "Shall we see if Tatelyn is all right?"

"I know she's all right," Simle said.

"Ah, of course. Well, walk with me so I may see for myself." Boy and dragon swiftly covered the distance to Yanna's cottage.

Ramma rose from her spot in the enlarged doorway and faced Molot and Simle. "Yanna told us of a pool that may give knowledge of the pendant. Tatelyn wishes to go there."

Molot whirled to his mother. "You told them of the pool? Why? That's a secret!"

"It's to be kept secret from those who would use it for harm," Yanna said calmly. "I know the importance of the pool even better than you, son. I think it'd be good for them."

Something unspoken passed between Yanna and Molot, but Simle couldn't imagine what it could be. But if this pool could tell them something about the pendant, perhaps they wouldn't even need to go to Palanthas. Simle could be free of Tatelyn much, much sooner.

"Take us there now!" Simle said, her tail quivering in excitement.

"No, not now," Yanna said, going over to Tatelyn. "Not until this girl here has a good night's rest." She examined Tatelyn's wounds and nodded. "Tomorrow, she can go."

That night, after a good sweeping, the humans slept in Yanna's cottage. Simle stayed by herself outside. She listened to them talking and laughing. Simle had never heard Tatelyn laugh before. The sound made her feel even lonelier.

Simle stared at the sky, mainly at the Platinum Dragon constellation. Could he see her? She missed other dragons terribly. As soon as she was free from Tatelyn, she would return home. Finding those humans her mother had protected no longer seemed important.

Simle flopped over on her side. A rock must have poked her because she heard Tatelyn yelp. Simle ignored her, wrapped up in her thoughts. Did her parents know what became of the eggs, that they were probably subjected to such a horrible fate? Was that why they fought the evil dragons alongside humans? Perhaps, Simle thought as she drifted to sleep, they fought to keep more eggs from being stolen.

The next morning, the four humans met Simle outside the cottage. Tatelyn appeared much improved, and Simle could tell from the lessened pain that Yanna knew her craft well. Simle knelt before Tatelyn.

"Here," she said, offering her back to Tatelyn.

The girl looked at her, then shook her head. "I don't need your help."

"Please?" Simle said quietly. Tatelyn flinched as though the dragon had shouted at her.

"Tatelyn, for Paladine's sake, let Simle carry you," Elrit said. "There's no need to be proud here."

"Fine," Tatelyn said and climbed atop Simle. Molot lead them to a large barn in the center of town.

"The pool is in a barn?" Tatelyn asked.

Molot smiled. "Not quite," he said as he opened the large barn door. Four people stood in the center of the barn, holding swords rather than hay rakes. Molot went to them and spoke quietly for a long time. The guards did not appear happy, but they finally moved aside, scraping hay away from the floor with their boots and revealing a large door set in the floor. Molot and the guards pulled a chain and the door swung up and open, revealing a large hole.

"The pool is in a cave deep in the mountain," Molot said, disappearing downward. A steep but walkable grade descended into darkness. "This is the easiest way to get there, and the reason the draconians tried to invade."

Simle looked at the others. They all shrugged, and Elrit and Ramma trailed Molot into the hole. Tatelyn slid off Simle's back and followed them. Simle poked her head down, relieved to see that the passage was large enough to accommodate a dragon much bigger than her once she squeezed through the hole.

"Keep close to me," Molot said as the cave floor leveled out. He pulled torches from a stack piled in the light from the barn above, lit them, and handed one torch to everyone. When he came to Simle, he looked at the torch and the dragon's clawed hands, bemused.

"My eyesight is a hundredfold better than yours, human," Simle said. "I need no torch."

Molot nodded and put the last torch back. "Stay close to me," he cautioned. "It might seem straightforward at first, but it's very easy to get lost in here."

Simle sniffed. "The day I get lost in a cave is the day I should curl into a ball and turn to stone."

Everyone chuckled, including Molot. "Still, stay close. We try to keep the caves free of any predators, but we still don't know all the ins and outs of this place."

Despite her words, Simle did find the caves strange, very unlike home. There was very little humidity and no sound of water save some occasional dripping stalactites. At first Simle was able to keep her bearings and could have, if needed, found her way out quickly. The deeper they traveled into the mountain, however, the more twists and turns the main path took, and soon Simle was completely confused. There seemed to be no pattern, but Molot strode through the tunnels as though it were the main path through Mountainhome.

"How do you know these tunnels so well?" Ramma asked. "I'd never be able to find my way back."

"All of us who guard the caves must know it. We're even tested while blindfolded."

"Just for this pool?" Elrit asked.

Molot did not answer, but looked up suddenly. Something skittered across the ceiling and vanished into the shadows.

"What was that?" Tatelyn whispered, drawing closer to Simle.

"I'm not sure," Molot said. He drew his sword. Elrit followed his example. "Be ready," Molot said. He handed daggers to Ramma and Tatelyn. "Something has found its way in."

"Draconians?" Simle asked. Molot shook his head.

"I don't think so. I couldn't see what that was, but I thought we drove them all off. Whatever it was, it came from the far side of the mountain, or above or below."

They had only taken a few more steps when three creatures dropped to the floor, one after the other. Draconians! This must be a different type. The creatures were much smaller than even Tatelyn and Ramma, and had a thin, reptilian appearance. They lacked the sophisticated armor the other draconians had, wearing scraps of leather armor and carrying crude spears and short swords instead.

"Try to get the small dragon. I hear they're good eating," one said in Draconic. Simle had trouble understanding them, as their Draconic sounded more like barking than speaking. Then she comprehended the meaning of the words. *Eating?*

A heavy weight landed on Simle's back. A fourth creature clung to her neck and began beating her about the head. She reared on her hind legs and it fell to the floor. It leaped to its feet and turned to face Simle, raising a spear.

"Kobolds!" Elrit exclaimed, running toward one with his sword raised.

Kobolds? Simle echoed in her mind. She'd never seen a kobold. A second look at the creatures made her realize that these beings could never have been dragons. The draconians, horrible as they were, had intelligence and skill. These were more like rodents. Not kin to me, Simle thought. Not now, not ever. She snapped her teeth at the kobold before her but it backed away more quickly than she expected. Molot and Elrit each faced one kobold, while another grinned at Ramma and Tatelyn.

"What is this?" it asked in a raspy voice. It eyed the girls. In that moment of hesitation, Ramma sent bolts of fire at the kobold. The bolts struck it and it crumpled to the ground, dead.

"Ow!" Tatelyn yelped as Simle's kobold leaped back

onto Simle's head and tried to stab her with its spear. Simle whipped her body back and forth, trying to get rid of the kobold, but it clung like a leech. Tatelyn raised her dagger and ran haltingly toward Simle. For a moment, Simle thought Tatelyn was going to plunge the weapon into Simle's eye. Then the weight on Simle's back slackened and fell off. Simle turned to face the kobold lying on the ground. Tatelyn had struck a good blow, planting her dagger in the kobold's thigh. It was far from finished, however. Simle grabbed its little body in her mouth and flung it away down the passage, where it crawled into a passage too narrow for Simle to follow.

"Did I get it?" Tatelyn asked, peering into the passage.

"Not entirely," Elrit said. "You maimed it pretty well, though. Where did you learn to do that?"

Tatelyn rubbed her head. "It's amazing what one can do when something is beating you about the head."

"The others?" Ramma asked.

Molot pointed to two dead kobolds farther up the cave and shook his head in disgust. "We find groups of them every so often. Most of the time they keep to themselves, but sometimes they decide to try something on us."

"Will that one return?" Tatelyn asked, looking in the direction the kobold she wounded had retreated.

"Not for a long time. Kobolds are easily scared off,

at least the ones I've run into here. If it does have friends here, it will have told them about us."

"Told them not to face us!" Elrit grinned, slapping Ramma and Tatelyn on the back. The girls smacked him back, but were smiling too. Simle did not feel happy at all. Even though they weren't draconians, their appearance had shaken her. Would anything remotely resembling a dragon make her think of her siblings forever?

As they resumed their pace through the cave, Molot said, "I'm not surprised the kobolds came here. The pool attracts many creatures, both good and evil. This is why we try to keep it as secret as possible. We already have enough on our hands without all Krynn knowing about it."

"I can see why," Elrit gasped, as they had entered a perfectly round room that deepened to a basin filled with what appeared to be molten gold. As they moved closer, Simle could see it was water that had a deep golden color.

"Stop," Molot said before any of them could touch the water. "Only the one who seeks the pool may approach." He turned to Tatelyn and Simle. "You must wade into the pool barefoot, my lady. Walk to the center, then look straight down."

Tatelyn looked at Molot uncertainly, then sat down on a rock to remove her well-worn leather shoes. Gathering her blue robes carefully in both hands, she waded into the pool. Simle waded after her, raising waves with every step. The pool was warm and soothing, but Simle couldn't tell if that was something she or Tatelyn felt. Probably both. At the center, the pool rose almost to Tatelyn's chest and Simle's upper legs. They stood there unmoving for a moment.

"Do we look together?" Simle asked Tatelyn.

"I guess so. On three?" Tatelyn counted, and they tilted their heads down and gazed into the pool.

The pool rushed toward Simle's face while simultaneously pulling her in, and she felt a sudden dizzy moment where up became down and down became up. As she regained her balance and looked around, she realized that she was no longer in the cave. She stood in a lush forest unlike any she had ever seen, the trees a strange bluish green color bursting with flowers and apples at the same time, and the sky a deep midnight blue. A voice called to her in Draconic, "Youngling!"

A dragon to talk to, at last! Overjoyed, Simle turned to see a large Silver female walking toward her. The silver dragon settled in front of Simle and smiled.

"I see you're learning about humans," the silver dragon said. "Rather interesting, aren't they?"

"Not at all," Simle said. "I'd be happier if I'd never met them."

The silver dragon's eyes clouded. "Then you must still be joined to this human. The good dragons and humans are very different, but they have much to offer each other. You will remain joined until you understand this lesson."

"No!" Simle cried as the silver dragon turned to walk away. "I have to be free of this human! I must return to my mother!"

The Silver's head swiveled back to look Simle deeply in the eye. "Why can't you return to your mother with the human?" she asked. "The human doesn't stop you. Look inward. You will learn much if you return to her."

"But we need to understand this pendant to end this spell!" Simle switched her tail like a whip, knocking apples from the tree she hit.

"You reach beyond the mark, little one. Understand the human, not the pendant. And be honest with the human as well as yourself." The silver dragon blinked once, and Simle felt the pull of the pool again. She rose out of the pool, gasping for breath. Tatelyn stood beside her, coughing up gold water.

"I hope you found out more than I did," Simle said as they waded out of the pool.

"A knight said I have to follow you to lift the spell." Tatelyn kicked at the water. "I learned nothing."

"A silver dragon told me we should go see my mother," Simle said.

Tatelyn was silent. Simle could almost hear the

thoughts tumbling in the girl's head. Surely she wouldn't want to enter a dragon's lair.

"It's ridiculous, but I'll follow you," Tatelyn said at last. "I think we need to listen to what the knight and dragon told us."

"Not so ridiculous," Molot said. "Follow me. I think I should show you something before we leave these caves." They traveled up a narrow passage slick with water that sparkled almost as much as the pool. Finally, they entered a warm circular chamber. Ten guards ringed the cave, all with spears or swords in hand. One guard stood beside a huge wood pile, stoking the huge fire that burned in the center of the room. Its light glinted off the specks of gold everywhere. The guards raised their weapons as soon as Molot entered the room, then put them down again when they recognized him.

"I thought it was time you all knew what the treasure of Mountainhome is," Molot said. "It's not the magical pool, although that is a treasure. Never before has an outsider seen this. But the pool spoke to both of you, and that tells me to trust you."

The room glittered even more brightly than the pool, a familiar brightness that Simle couldn't place. In that fire, a cluster of objects shone brighter than the fire. Once her eyes adjusted to the light, Simle knew what they were. She cried out.

"Eggs!" Elrit exclaimed, looking sideways at Tatelyn. "Dragon eggs!"

"A gold dragon came to Mountainhome during the war. She needed a place to lay her eggs, and this was the only cave she found suitable. She was still here when the draconians attacked. She defended us, but she had already been weakened in a battle farther north." Molot's jaw quivered. "Before she died, she told some of us where her eggs were hidden and asked that we keep them in the open flame, because that's the only way a gold dragon's eggs will ever hatch. All who swore to protect them took the name Auricwatch from that day forward."

Simle could no longer bear it. She collapsed on the floor of the chamber, sobbing.

"It's all my fault!" Simle said. "It wouldn't have happened if I hadn't been so silly!"

"The gold dragon dying?" Tatelyn asked, her violet eyes wide. "You weren't even here for that!"

"Not that!" Simle cried. "My siblings! They're gone because of me. They were stolen and turned into draconians because of me!"

Chapter Seventeen

I was just a hatchling. I saw a sparkly gem and I couldn't resist chasing it as it rolled away. It was more beautiful than any pearl I ever saw. When I found my way back to the nest, all the eggs were gone." Simle drew a deep, shuddering breath. "I never saw my siblings again. But I may have seen them recently."

"The draconians," Molot gasped, looking at the golden eggs. "Bozacs. They were made from bronze dragon eggs, weren't they?"

Simle nodded. "No one ever told me why the eggs were taken. They just said it was evil humans. I thought that my siblings were killed, or maybe even alive somewhere. To find them changed into those creatures . . ." Her eyes filled with tears again. Ramma produced a handkerchief and offered it to Simle. Simle looked blankly at the tiny piece of lace.

"Here," Ramma said, and reached out to dab the dragon's eyes. Molot pulled her back and indicated the stone below

Simle. Ramma saw the tears sizzling holes into the stone, gasped, and took a step back.

Simle's tale filled Tatelyn with sadness and confusion. Once, she would have thought that such a fate was just what a dragon—any dragon—deserved. Now, hearing the huge creature sobbing with a grief that would have seemed ridiculous had it not been so sorrowful, she felt pity. Until now, Simle had been at best an annoyance, someone Tatelyn must bear until they could part ways. Most of the time, Tatelyn still burned with a deep anger whenever she looked upon this creature, so like the one that aided in her brother's death. Now, for the first time, she felt sorrow for Simle.

"It's a sad story," Molot said, reaching up to touch Simle's head while carefully avoiding the tears. "But it's very common. That happened to so many dragons before the war. It's why we guard these eggs so carefully, so the same fate won't befall them. It's not your fault, or your parents' fault, or any other good dragon's fault. Who could have anticipated that the Dark Queen's agents would steal the eggs of good dragons? The good dragons had been promised that no harm would come to their eggs if they stayed out of the war, but now we know what a horrendous lie that was."

"Your parents surely didn't know there was danger back then," Ramma pointed out. "Would they have been sleeping if they thought any danger might come to you?"

"I suppose not," Simle said, wiping her eyes with the back of her talon. "Can we go now?" she said, sounding very childish. For the first time, Tatelyn wondered how old Simle was in dragon years. Right now she sounded no more than eight years old. "I want to see my mother." She took one last, longing look at the golden eggs, then walked back down the passage.

Molot ran ahead of her to lead the way out of the caves. As the rest of them followed, Elrit asked, "What makes the water gold?"

"The eggs," Molot said. "Some of the gold flakes off and as it falls into the stream, it flows to the golden pool. We think that the eggs will be ready to hatch soon, actually—it takes about two years, but they've been flaking more lately, and we see a little movement sometimes."

"The pool hasn't always been here?" Ramma asked, slipping on the wet stones and regaining her balance.

"No, it was always here," Molot said. "It wasn't until the golden dragon laid her eggs that it turned to gold and developed magical powers. Some people think that it was the dragon's last gift to us, as thanks for protecting her children."

Tatelyn liked that idea. Perhaps Simle's mother would do the same thing. Going to a dragon's lair seemed very foolish and very dangerous, but it might be the only way to find out more about the pendant. And if we find out no more there, Tatelyn told herself, we can go back to Palanthas. Elistan knows *something* about this.

They returned through the caves swiftly. Tatelyn shuddered as they passed the kobold bodies. She looked for the one she had stabbed, but it was gone. Never before had she attacked any creature—now she'd attacked two in as many days. It felt terrible to harm instead of heal. Even with the dragons, she sought only their banishment. For the first time, Tatelyn wondered what would happen if they couldn't get the dragons to agree to leave. Would that mean another war?

As soon as they returned to the village, Tatelyn and the others busied themselves preparing for the journey. Yanna prepared bags for all of them with plenty of dried rations. Ramma offered to pay her for them, but the woman refused to take money. With a rare wink at Tatelyn, Ramma hid a small bag of steel in a clay pot.

Molot sat down with them and sketched a quick map in the dirt to show them the surrounding area. Simle thought she could find her parents' home once they reached the bay—all they would need to do was follow the sea.

"A few days' journey at least," Ramma sighed. "Why did I leave the caravan?"

"We can't spare a wagon, but we can give you horses," Yanna said. "That'll help."

Ramma tucked even more steel about Yanna's house while Tatelyn and Elrit got acquainted with the horses. Tatelyn expected the horses to be nervous around Simle, but they barely seemed to notice her. Perhaps the horses had grown accustomed to the gold dragon back when she was here.

The journey was much easier for Tatelyn now that she had the company of her friends. When they made camp that evening, Simle forced Tatelyn to sit down and rest.

"I'm not tired," Tatelyn objected, conscious of how petulant she sounded. She felt as though she could walk for days.

"You are," Simle insisted. "My every bone aches from this long journey and my hand still hurts. It's not like you're completely healed yet. If we are attacked, your pain will distract me from fighting."

The dragon had a point. If Simle was feeling Tatelyn's pain that bad, Tatelyn might hurt herself without knowing it. So Tatelyn sat quietly, watching Simle, Ramma, and Elrit make a fire and look for food. When Simle returned with a small deer, a debate began over whether Tatelyn should eat the meat cooked, as she wanted, or raw, which Simle swore was better for dragons.

"I will rest when you ask, but I am *not* eating raw meat!" Tatelyn said with a shudder.

"Humans," Simle grumbled through a mouthful of

meat. Ramma and Elrit looked at Tatelyn and grimaced.

That night, they decided that Elrit would keep watch the first part of the night, then Simle, and last Ramma. Tatelyn wanted a watch as well since she still wasn't tired, but Simle threatened to tie her to the ground and clamp her eyes shut if Tatelyn didn't rest. So Tatelyn stared at the stars and listened to the dragon snoring next to her until she fell asleep.

In the morning, they resumed their journey. Used to traveling the roads, Tatelyn found it strange they didn't encounter anyone, but it suited Simle just fine. The dragon even sang a bit as they came within sight of the water. The song was peculiarly catchy, but Tatelyn kept her distance even when Ramma and Elrit began to sing with Simle.

On the third day, they finally saw some humans. Elrit spotted them first. "Off to the side of the road!" he said, but Simle didn't move.

"They wear robes like Tatelyn's," she said. "Only white. Three of them."

Clerics of Paladine? Shortly Tatelyn saw the clerical robes Simle described. "Human?" she asked Simle.

"It appears so," the dragon said. "Shall we continue?"

"Yes," Tatelyn said. "But be careful."

Suddenly, one of the clerics pointed toward the party. Moments later, all of them were running toward the companions, shouting and making the horses shy.

Even though it didn't look as much like an attack as a seizure, Elrit drew his bow on them and Ramma began murmuring words of a defensive spell just in case.

"Hold!" shouted Tatelyn. "What do you want?" The clerics, all women, Tatelyn now saw, rushed past her, Elrit, and Ramma and skidded to a halt in front of a very puzzled Simle.

"Is it truly you?" one of the women asked. The others seemed too overwhelmed to speak.

Simle managed a quizzical look at the woman.

"You wear the Starjewel," the woman said. "That means your mother made her way back to you. Is she all right?"

"How do you know my mother?" Simle croaked. Tatelyn saw that her bronze color seemed to have dulled, even though they stood in bright sunshine.

"She saved us," the woman said. "A party of us made a pilgrimage to Huma's tomb, all the way out on the island of Southern Ergoth."

"It was you?" Simle gasped. "You were the people she protected?" The dragon's voice was barely above a whisper.

The woman didn't seem to notice the effect she had on Simle. She babbled on, "She saved us when we were attacked by a black dragon. We had nothing to give her but that jewel. None of us had the power to heal her, much to our dismay." The woman reached out a thin white finger and touched the Starjewel gently. Simle flinched. "When you see your mother, tell her that Winsa hopes she is doing well and finds much happiness in her life."

Simle nodded, speechless. Tatelyn wasn't sure what was going through Simle's mind, but if Simle wasn't going to ask, she would. When Simle slumped to the ground without answering Winsa, the woman gestured to the other clerics, and they turned to continue their journey with many well wishes. Before they could go, Tatelyn slid off her horse and shouted, "Wait!"

This time the women saw her. Winsa slowed as the other two looked back from farther down the road.

"Can you tell us anything about the Starjewel?" Tatelyn asked, running to the woman.

"We found the broken piece in Huma's tomb, right next to the Monument of the Silver Dragon," Winsa said. "We were going to leave it there—we didn't want to plunder. But one of our group, a very wise woman with the gift of prophesy, dreamed that we were to give that to the first dragon we saw. That was this young dragon's mother, may Paladine bless her."

"Which woman had the dream?" Ramma asked. She seemed deep in thought, as though putting pieces of a puzzle together.

"A very strange one. She parted with us on the road soon after," Winsa said, gesturing toward her companions. "I haven't seen her since we left the tomb, actually. She was lovely, with long silver hair. Good day to you, great one." She bowed to Simle. "We must hurry along before night falls." With a bow and a nod, Winsa followed her group away.

"Silver hair," Ramma whispered, looking at Simle's Starjewel. "Could it be possible?"

"What does silver hair have to do with it?" Tatelyn asked.

"When a silver dragon takes human form," Simle said, "they often have silver hair. And didn't you tell me that Huma loved a silver dragon?"

Tatelyn shivered. She turned to look for the clerics to try to get their attention one last time, but they had vanished over the horizon.

CHAPTER EIGHTEEN

I had them, Simle thought, hanging her head in shame. They were right there in front of me, and I didn't do a thing.

The meeting with the clerics weighed on Simle's mind as they approached home. Once, those humans were all that she thought about, all she wanted to find after leaving home. But coming face-to-face with them, seeing their joy and gratitude upon meeting her, made Simle powerless. She could barely say a word to them, let alone accuse them of causing her mother's injuries.

Those clerics were not the same as the Heirs of Huma, Simle realized. Not if they went to the Monument of the Silver Dragon that guarded Huma's tomb. Those women were victims of circumstance, as was she, as was her mother. She couldn't hold them responsible for the actions of a black dragon.

Simle was so wrapped up in her own thoughts that it wasn't until they finally reached the entrance that she realized there was a problem—a problem so glaringly obvious, yet so much a part of Simle's life that she never once thought it would be an issue.

"We have to what?" Tatelyn gasped, looking over the edge of the cliff. The horses cropped the grass contentedly nearby, unaware or uncaring of the sheer plunge.

"Swim to my home." Simle slapped her tail against the ground, sending a rattling stream of pebbles into the water below. "I can't believe I forgot."

"What's the problem?" Elrit asked, leaning over the edge of the cliff. "You go in, we wait out here. You talk to your father, come back out and get us. Easy."

"No, not that easy," Simle said, frowning at the water. "How deep can humans swim?"

"Not very," Tatelyn said. Her eyes locked with Simle's and for one moment, each knew the other's thoughts perfectly. "It will be the same as flying, won't it?"

"I'm afraid so." Simle looked at the water in frustration. "You can't go, Tatelyn," Simle said. "You'll never find the way."

Tatelyn sat down at the edge of the cliff, dangling her legs over the sea far below. "Now what? How can we get to your parents?"

"Ever think of trying another way?" asked a new voice.

Everyone looked around, but could see no one.

Simle thought she recognized the voice, however. "Uncle Nuvar?"

"The same!"

"Where are you?" Simle looked around. "This is no time for jokes!"

Tatelyn yelped and scrambled back from the cliff edge. "Something grabbed my ankle!"

Chuckling, Uncle Nuvar, in human form, emerged from below the edge of the cliff. "I never could resist a pretty girl." He stood and brushed dust off his green cloak.

"*You're* Simle's uncle?" Tatelyn gaped at the man. "But you're human!"

"All bronze dragons can polymorph, my dear. This one, though"—he gestured to Simle—"has some rather silly prejudices against humans."

"We can discuss that later," Simle said. "I need to see my parents, but I can't get to the cave." As quickly as they could, Simle and Tatelyn told Uncle Nuvar about their link.

"I have heard of such things, though never one such as this," he said, peering at the jewels that girl and dragon wore. "I wish I could tell you something of it, but your mother hasn't spoken a word since you left." Uncle Nuvar glared at Simle. "It was a very foolish thing you did, leaving like that. What were you thinking?"

Simle tried to recall, bowing her head meekly. At

the time she left, she wanted only to hurt humans as they had hurt her mother. She looked at the three people she now traveled with: two human girls and one half-elf boy.

"Never mind," Uncle Nuvar sighed. "There's a way into the mountain that humans can take, though we keep it well hidden. Follow me."

Uncle Nuvar led them down a path down the opposite side of the hill that Simle had never seen. She had always used the underwater entrance.

"I see you have at least learned to tolerate humans," he said to Simle, who didn't reply. "There are other dragons who are beginning to think as you, though. There was a conclave called to discuss a new movement among some of the humans. Some of them wish for the good dragons to leave these lands."

Simle glanced back at the others. She saw them exchange a somewhat guilty, somewhat embarrassed look. But the Heirs of Huma wasn't as important as straightening out the jewel mess. It was just too complicated.

"Ah, here we are." Uncle Nuvar stopped in front of a boulder that would take ten men to move. He changed from his human form back to dragon and rolled the boulder aside before Tatelyn, Ramma, and Elrit could finish their shocked gasps.

"Just follow the passage." Uncle Nuvar gestured into

the tunnel with a flourish. "Simle, you should be able to fit. I'll return shortly."

"You aren't coming with us?" Simle asked.

"I need to go to that conclave and find out what those humans are up to. Don't they know not to tweak a sleeping dragon's tail?" With those final words, Uncle Nuvar leaped into the air and took off.

"See what you caused?" Simle asked Tatelyn.

"I can't do anything about that now," Tatelyn said, entering the tunnel. "Let's just fix this thing first."

Simle agreed, though she didn't like it. She entered last and tried to move the boulder back into place, but couldn't budge it.

"I wish Uncle Nuvar would have waited until we were inside to leave," she grunted.

"I don't," Ramma shuddered. "How would we get out?"

Simle left the boulder open, although she really wished she was strong enough to move it. Something about leaving an easy entry into her home open made her feel uneasy.

This passage was much easier to follow than the one at Mountainhome. There were no off-shooting passages, no damp areas to trip them, no kobolds. Before long, a sighing echoed through the tunnel.

Tateyn jumped. "What was that?"

"Either my mother or father," Simle said, her heart filling with joy. "They must be sleeping." If her mother was in serious harm, her father wouldn't sleep. She picked up speed, running down the tunnel, ducking the occasional low-hanging rock, but pulled up short when she hit a big, blank wall.

"Who's there?" a thunderous voice called. "Do you know where you tread?"

Tatelyn, Ramma, and Elrit froze.

"It's me, Father!" Simle called. "How do we get out of this passage?"

"Simle? Is it really you?"

Simle heard a few muffled words of magic, then an opening appeared. Beyond it, her father stood waiting. She yelped with joy and ran straight into him.

"You're all right!" her father said, nuzzling her. "Don't run off again!"

"How is Mother?" Simle asked. Her mother lay where she had last seen her, but her breathing seemed to be easier.

"Resting now," Simle's father said. "She needs deep sleep to heal and must not be disturbed. She is not going to leave us, though."

Simle collapsed on the floor in relief.

"Why do I smell humans?" her father asked, turning toward the tunnel where the three others huddled. "Come forward if you mean us no harm." Slowly, they obeyed, trembling under Father's stern gaze.

"You travel with humans?" Father asked Simle, his eyes wide in amazement.

Simle looked at the ground. "It's a very long story, too long to tell now. First, what do you know of this?" Simle held up the Starjewel. "Mother gave it to me when she returned."

"I don't know anything about it," Father said, holding the jewel in the light. "She had it with her when I found her, and I didn't have time to ask her where she found it or anything. You know as much as I do."

Simle's head sagged. Tatelyn slumped beside her. When would they finally be able to get answers?

Simle's father's eyes suddenly widened and he shoved Simle over to the side. Simle stumbled and cried out as a net enveloped her father. Through the tunnel came a band of humans, one of them dressed in shiny metal.

"Simle, don't fight them!" her father called, struggling in the net. "They're led by a Knight of Solamnia! We're their allies!"

"Allies," said the knight. "Hardly." He turned to Tatelyn, Ramma, and Elrit. "It's all right. We've come to rescue you."

Chapter Nineteen

ogan! Tatelyn relaxed. Of course they must have tracked them here. But why hadn't they revealed themselves sooner?

"Horao and Poal, chain the beasts," Rogan commanded as he pointed his sword at Simle and her father. Simle's father bowed his head and allowed Horao, who had once chided Tatelyn and Marin for stealing apples from his orchard, to wrap chains around his mighty legs and neck. Why won't he fight? Tatelyn wondered. He could easily kill all of these humans. Rogan had brought ten or so fighting men, all Heirs of Huma and about half of them people she knew from Forestedge.

Tatelyn felt a tightening around her wrists. Simle was being shackled by Poal, one of Rogan's younger friends, whose hands visibly shook. Simle looked at Tatelyn, her eyes filled with resignation. She knew she couldn't fight without hurting Tatelyn. Tatelyn winced as another chain was wrapped around Simle's back leg. The dragon looked so hopeless. Not once since they met had Tatelyn seen her look so downcast.

"Wait!" she cried, running toward Poal. "Please, let her go!" But rather than obeying her at once, Poal looked to Rogan for confirmation.

Shock washed over Rogan's face in a wave. He nodded to the knight Loran, who stood by watching the others shackle the dragons. Loran grabbed Tatelyn's arms and held them behind her back before she realized what was happening. Fear gripped Tatelyn's heart, not just for Simle, but for herself. Elrit was quickly restrained as well.

"Rogan! What are you doing?" Ramma gaped at her brother. "Let Tatelyn and Elrit go! For that matter, release the dragons! They've done us no harm."

Pain creased Rogan's brow. "They enchanted you too, then." He twitched a finger at Keel, the Forestedge baker's apprentice. Keel pulled a length of cloth taut between her hands as she darted behind Ramma.

"Ramma, look out!" Tatelyn cried too late as Keel wrapped the cloth around Ramma's head. Tatelyn's heart stopped. Surely Ramma was going to be strangled. Then she realized that the cloth was only to gag the wizard so she couldn't cast spells. Ramma struggled for a moment, then relaxed when it was clear she wasn't in mortal danger—at least not yet.

Why was no one fighting?

Simle's father spoke to the knights in a low, rumbling voice. "I will go with you peacefully, honored knights. I have fought beside your kind before. I will not harm any of you."

"Don't listen to the beast," Rogan barked. "It will enchant you as it has our friends."

"We're not enchanted!" Tatelyn snapped. "Why won't you listen?"

Rogan patted Tatelyn's arm condescendingly. "When we find a way to break the enchantment, you'll return to your old self, as will my sister and Elrit." Rogan glared at Elrit. "If you wanted to rescue Tatelyn, you should have gone alone."

Ramma's eyes flashed like blue fire. Tatelyn could imagine the snide remark that would have shot from Ramma had she not been gagged.

"Please don't hurt the dragon," Tatelyn said. "Anything you do to her, I feel."

"So that's how she holds you in thrall," said Loran. "Interesting."

"Enough talk," Rogan said. "We must secure the beasts. What about that one?" He pointed to Simle's mother.

"Leave her alone!" Simle roared, struggling against the chains.

"Looks ill, sir," said one of men, examining the large female. "What are your orders?"

Rogan walked about the cave, looking it over carefully. Tatelyn noticed that he took care to stay well out of reach of all the dragons. "We'll stay here for now," he finally said. "It appears that the only entrances to this cave are the one we came through and that one." Rogan gestured to a large, downward-sloping tunnel at the other end of the cave.

That must be the tunnel that exits to the sea, Tatelyn thought.

"You, dragon!" Rogan marched up to Simle's father even though the dragon towered over him. It was a ridiculous sight. Tatelyn would have laughed if the circumstances were not so serious.

"Are those the only ways into this cave?" Rogan asked. Simle's father said nothing. Rogan frowned, drew his sword, and banged the flat of it against the dragon's tree trunk of a leg.

Simle's father still said nothing, but looked down at Rogan with sparkling eyes. If his tears were like Simle's, Rogan had best move before one fell on him. The large Bronze blinked quickly, and the tears vanished. Finally, he said in a low voice, "Yes."

Rogan seemed satisfied. "Watch the dragons carefully," he told the others. "I'll take my sister, Tatelyn, and

Elrit to the surface and return shortly."

"Are you going to hurt them?" Tatelyn asked, struggling to keep her voice firm.

"They're worth more to us alive," Rogan said. Tatelyn went limp with relief and would have fallen to the ground were it not for the strong arms still holding her.

"Don't you remember the plan?" Rogan asked Tatelyn. "We hoped to capture one dragon. Three is much better. Now the rest of the metallic dragons will be forced to listen to us." Rogan suddenly clamped his mouth shut and glanced at the dragons. Simle and her father remained motionless. "Let's talk elsewhere. Loran, Poal, and Britaw, bring the prisoners with me."

Tatelyn managed one last look at Simle as they were hurried back into the tunnel. She mouthed to the dragon, "I'll save you." Simle looked surprised, then bobbed her head slightly. Tatelyn hoped that once they had a chance to sit and talk with Rogan, he might be persuaded to let the dragons go.

That hope faded with every step they took toward the surface. Rogan simply refused to listen to anything Tatelyn or Elrit had to say about the dragons. Rogan refused to ungag his sister.

"How could you go off on your own, Ramma?" he berated her. "We needed you!"

Ramma still could say nothing, but Elrit spoke for

her. "Tatelyn needed her more," Elrit retorted. "You were willing to abandon her!"

"Tatelyn would have agreed with me," Rogan said, turning to Tatelyn. "You've always said that the mission of the Heirs of Huma comes before the people."

"Yes, but that was before!" Tatelyn said, annoyed at having her own words flung back at her. "I've spent a lot of time with this dragon. She means us no harm. And any pain inflicted upon her, I feel."

Rogan burst out laughing. It was a strange sound, echoing through the tunnel. Tatelyn couldn't remember a time when she saw him laugh—and found it disturbing. "It's a slippery dragon," he said, "to take the leader of the Heirs of Huma and make her believe such a thing."

"You don't believe me?" Tatelyn gasped. "Why would I tell you such a thing? Ask Elrit! Ask Ramma! They saw what happens!"

"I am sure they did," Rogan said. "Dragons possess very powerful magic. It's child's play for them to enchant you and make you say such lies."

"But she has no magic!" Tatelyn exclaimed, feeling as though she were back with the draconians. She probably could have convinced them more easily than Rogan, the hard-headed nut. "When we became linked, she lost her magic and I lost my clerical powers!"

"Don't you think the dragon would want you to

believe that?" Rogan spoke to Tatelyn as though she were a very small child. It made Tatelyn want to smack him. He'd truly lost it. "Really, Tatelyn, I'm surprised at you," Rogan said. "Your brother was killed by a copper dragon."

"They aren't Copper, they're Bronze!" Tatelyn snapped.

Rogan shrugged. "I should've known even that reason wouldn't break through a spell," he said. "Once we kill the young one, there will be no further problems."

"No!" Tatelyn struggled but could not break free. They dragged her and her friends out of the cave entrance and up the hill. The cliff overlooking the water was no longer empty. All the Heirs of Huma were there, setting up camp. Rogan went to Tatelyn and Ramma's wagon, opened the door, and the guards pushed Ramma, Tatelyn, and Elrit in.

"Perhaps we should kill the little one now?" asked Intar, one of Rogan's friends.

Rogan considered, then shook his head. "We still need them for bargaining. We may be forced to send all three dragons' heads at some point, but we should at least see what the Whitestone Council has to say first. Guard them," he said to Loran, Poal, and Britaw, who nodded gravely.

Rogan was more clever than Tatelyn had realized. He knew she might appeal to anyone from Forestedge and could talk them into letting her go, so he had chosen people not from there.

"Don't get too close, though, in case the dragon's spell should move from them to you," Rogan instructed, walking back to the tunnel entrance.

The guards bound the three of them with ropes, then left them sitting in the wagon. From the sounds outside, they didn't go far.

"The dragons won't give in to threats," Elrit said. "Simle's father won't fight now, but if they try to kill him or his family, I'm sure he will. Once the other metallic dragons hear of this, they'll declare war on the Heirs of Huma. We could very well have another war, only this time *no* dragons will be on our side."

Tatelyn shuddered. "That would be horrible, but what if they decide to kill Simle anyway, to break the spell? Do I die too?"

Elrit set his jaw. "We have to find a way out of here."

CHAPTER TWENTY

Fear and worry twisted Simle's stomach as she scanned the people in the cave. There were only a handful, but her father's quick surrender frightened her more than a hundred humans.

"Why didn't you fight?" Simle asked her father in Draconic so none of the humans could understand. She drew as close to him as the chains would let her. "My magic is gone, but *you* could've flattened them with one breath."

"I can't attack them," Father said. "We worked too long and too hard to get humans to trust us. I've fought to protect humans. Attacking them would mean that Takhisis and the evil dragons have won."

"But we might die!" Simle said, near tears. "We should defend ourselves."

"Perhaps." Simle's father scanned the humans. "But we must wait to see their plans."

"I have learned much of this group of humans," Simle

said. "They hate dragons, all dragons. This group dedicates itself to banishing the metallic dragons from Krynn."

Simle's father chuckled. "And how, precisely, do they seek to accomplish that?"

"I'm not sure, but I believe it has something to do with them capturing us. This same group tried to capture me. That's how I met Tatelyn."

"Tatelyn is with these people?" Simle's father looked in the direction they had taken her. "They sure didn't act like friends."

Simle took a deep breath. The time to tell her father was now. "Tatelyn is leader of these people." She then braced for the explosion.

Father was so surprised for a moment he looked blank. Then his mouth opened and he began roaring—not with fury, but with laugher.

"Oh, the gods do have a sense of humor," he said, slapping his tail against the ground. "To bind my daughter, with her anti-human sentiments, to a human who hates dragons." The guards around them shifted their weapons, alarmed at the dragon's strange noises. "Is this something you and she planned together? Something that would force the dragons to leave Krynn? I knew you were a clever dragon, my dear, but this?"

"No!" Simle gasped. "Tatelyn and I just want to break the curse. It—"

"Is there even a curse?" her father guffawed. "These humans are no threat!" he exclaimed. "They won't hurt me! I think I'll give them something to remember me!" Picking out an older man wearing a white robe, he called in Common, "You there! Yes, you, with the silly looking beard."

The man raised a hand to his chin with a hurt look.

"What would you do if I started something like this?" Simle's father took a deep breath and sent lightning crackling loudly but harmlessly across the top of the cave. The humans screamed and huddled on the ground, arms flung over their heads. As shocked as Simle was that her father would scare humans, she did wonder how the humans thought mere weapons would protect them if they were struck by lightning.

After the lightning died away, the humans scrambled to their feet. The man with the beard, which *was* rather silly looking with its long curls, pointed a hand at Simle's father and shouted, *"Ente tidur!"*

Simle's father blinked heavily. He swayed back and forth like he did when he ate too much of Uncle Nuvar's special dragon broth. He shuddered and collapsed on the floor with a thud that shook the cavern.

"Father!" Simle cried, straining to get closer. The white wizard seemed to consider her, then must have decided she was no threat. Simle stretched her neck so she could look her father in the eye.

"Father," she cried again. "Are you all right?"

Her father mumbled incoherently. His eyes were open, revealing pupils so dilated that little remained of the bronze outer color.

"Sleep spell," he managed, sounding as though his mouth were stuffed with jellyfish. "White wizard attack. Why?"

"Father, stay awake! I need your help!"

Her father struggled to keep his eyes open. "Spell powerful. Took me by surprise. Stupid."

"Fight it," Simle said, fighting back tears. If Father fell asleep along with Mother, she would have no one. "Please don't leave me alone."

Muttering, Father propped himself up on his front legs. Simle could not reach him to help, so she stared at him, wishing her gaze could give him strength. He leaned against the cave wall, breathing heavily.

Simle's mind raced to think everything out one more time. She thought of Tatelyn and the hatred she saw in the girl's eyes. While Simle no longer thought the girl hated her with such a blind ferocity, she harbored no illusions that once they broke this link, they would go their separate ways. A thought then struck Simle and made her gasp.

"Tatelyn tried to capture me before. What if this is a ploy?" Fear and anger raced through Simle like fire.

"I don't follow," Father said sleepily. Simle wanted her regular father back, the one who could piece together puzzles and plots lightning quick.

"Everything about this switch has disadvantaged me more than her," Simle realized. "So what if Tatelyn can't heal. She feels my hurt, but with my scales, I don't get hurt as much as she does. But it convinces me we have to travel together, and since her body can't withstand flying, I'm grounded. I can't swim, or do magic, or even talk to animals."

Everything that had happened was clicking together in Simle's mind with horrifying efficiency. "She tricked me," Simle gasped. "They must have followed me, seen my gem, and come up with some way to switch us. Inconvenient for her, true, but she would do anything to further her cause!"

"Slow down, young one," her father mumbled. "You are ascribing quite a plot for such a young human girl."

"You don't know her, Father," Simle said. "She's so driven. All these people"—Simle flicked her tail about—"all of them are here because of her."

"She may have set something in motion that she didn't fully understand at the time," her father said thickly. "Don't judge her harshly. And you must keep one question in mind."

"What?" Simle wanted to roar with frustration, but knew that would attract too much attention.

"What happens if you die? Or if Tatelyn dies? The link is real—you seem to be convinced of that. That is the one aspect that no one can fully understand until it's too late."

Simle forced herself to calm down and focus on her father's words. While his sympathy for humans had always grated upon her, he did have a point. There were just too many things she didn't know.

Simle looked at her mother, who was still sound asleep. "She never said anything about this jewel? Are you sure?"

"Not a word," her father said.

"We can't wake her up?"

"Even if she'd rested enough, which she hasn't, I wouldn't wake her up." Father's gaze flickered around the cave. "They're afraid. They'd be more afraid if they had two grown dragons to face, not just one. Fearful humans are dangerous."

"Fear," Simle murmured. Fear was what had driven Tatelyn to create the Heirs of Huma, she realized. It seemed like hate, but really, it was fear—fear that the dragons would come back and harm her family and friends again.

Simle was no different. There was just one thing she hadn't mentioned yet to her father about her journey.

"Why didn't you tell me about draconians?" she asked softly.

Her father's sagging eyes snapped wide open. "Where did you hear that word?"

"I met some. They captured Tatelyn, tortured her. I fought them, even though they said they were kin." Simle looked her father straight in the eye. "Is this true?"

Simle's father bowed his head. "It is. We were going to tell you when you were older. It happened to many dragon families. Eggs were stolen and, through some of the blackest rites ever performed, were perverted into those creatures."

"Why didn't you try to get the eggs back?" Simle asked, stricken. "I assumed they were dead!"

"So did we, for a long time. Once we found out what was going on, it was too late. I heard a tale of some gold and silver dragons who tried to reclaim their children, but it was impossible. We had to accept their loss and take joy in the one thing we had left." Simle's father reached out the tip of his tail and touched Simle's tail. "You."

Father's head drooped. "Their spell is getting to be too much for me," he said.

"Please don't leave me alone," Simle whispered. "I can't do this on my own."

"You have other friends," her father said, curling his body tightly on the floor. His breathing deepened. "You'll find a way," he murmured so low Simle could barely hear. Then he finally drifted into a deep sleep.

CHAPTER TWENTY-ONE

"Well, this is a fine mess," Tatelyn grumbled to Ramma and Elrit. "Captured by our own people!" Tatelyn scooched over to Ramma. She inched up the wall until she was standing, then turned to ungag Ramma. It took a few moments because she couldn't see the knots she was untying, but at last Ramma's mouth was free.

"My brother always knew he couldn't win an argument with me, even before I began my magical studies," Ramma fumed. "I guess he figured out a way to shut me up."

Elrit wiggled, working at the rope tying his hands behind him. "I should have these untied soon."

"Then what?" Tatelyn asked, leaning her head against the wagon wall with a thump. "We have to deal with all the guards. How am I supposed to convince them that I'm not under any spell?"

Elrit and Ramma both looked meaningfully at Tatelyn.

"All right," she amended. "Not under any spell that controls my *mind*." For a moment, she had forgotten the spell that bound her to Simle. She hadn't felt any pain for a while, so she hoped that meant Simle was doing all right.

Elrit craned his neck to look at the ceiling. "Do you think they're looking at the wagon roof? Perhaps I could slip out the top."

Tatelyn and Ramma looked up. A small door that they opened when the weather was nice was set in the ceiling.

"And where are you planning on going once you're on the roof?" Ramma asked. "Or did you figure out how to become invisible?"

Elrit grinned as he slipped one wrist out of the ropes. "Actually," he said, "I have."

A few moments later, Tatelyn began hollering for the guards as loud as she could. Ramma lay slumped on the floor, eyes closed. Elrit was nowhere in sight.

"Guards! Guards! Please come! Something's wrong with Ramma!"

Keys rattled at the door the moment Tatelyn mentioned Ramma. Of course, she thought with an inward sigh. Even though I'm the leader of the Heirs of Huma, I am, after all, a farm girl. Ramma's good looks matched her equally rich clothes, and all the men in the Heirs of Huma had made eyes at her.

The guards finally got the door unlocked and burst in. Their eyes widened when they saw Lady Ramma, daughter of one of the most prominent Solamnic families, lying like a crumpled rag on the floor.

"What happened?" Intar gasped.

"We've been locked in here for hours, no fresh air, no water. What did you expect to happen?" Tatelyn snapped. "Untie her at once!"

"W-we can't do that—" Britaw stammered. The taller, slightly older man, a well-to-do farmer they'd recruited from a village halfway between Forestedge and Palanthas, fidgeted with his sword hilt.

"Do you want to be the one to explain to Sir Rogan that his sister lay unconscious while you did nothing?" Tatelyn glared at the guards, who looked at each other, then at Ramma's body. Intar shut the wagon door and stood in front of it while Britaw went to Ramma.

"Lady Crownguard?" He put a gentle hand on her shoulder. Ramma rolled limply over, her face pale and eyes closed. Britaw frowned through his ginger-colored beard. "What happened before she fainted?" he asked Tatelyn as he lightly patted Ramma's cheeks.

"She said the walls were closing in around her," Tatelyn said, raising her voice to cover the soft thump above her. "Then she just collapsed. She needs to be untied and she needs fresh air!"

"You're a cleric. Can't you do anything here?" Intar asked, leaning against the door as though he expected the two girls to make a run for it. He glanced around, looking puzzled. "Weren't there three in here?"

Britaw looked up, alarmed. Something fell from the ceiling, knocking him down. Intar moved toward him, but Tatelyn rose, the ropes falling loosely from her wrists, and hit Intar in the head with one of Ramma's books.

"Be careful with that!" Ramma said, rising from the floor, her hands freed as well. "That's one of my favorites."

"Now it's done us all a great favor," Elrit said, rising from Britaw. "Is he out?"Tatelyn checked both knights and nodded. "Out cold," she said. She eyed both of them, then looked Elrit up and down. "Take Intar's armor. He's about your size."

Elrit stripped Intar of his armor while Ramma and Tatelyn tied up the older knight. Ramma gagged him with a silk scarf as Tatelyn helped Elrit into the armor.

"I always knew the knights were crazy for wearing this much armor," Elrit grumbled, trying to figure out the buckles. "No wonder it takes them forever to make a decision."

"Here, let me do it." Ramma rose and helped Elrit strap the plate mail on over the chain-mail shirt, then pulled a helmet over his head, hiding his eyes and ears. "I've seen Rogan and Father do this before." Ramma fastened the last buckle as Tatelyn opened the door. The three of them stepped out, blinking in the bright sunlight. The guards circling the wagon all pointed their weapons, then lowered them when they saw that Tatelyn and Ramma were accompanied by a guard. Elrit supported Ramma as though she still had trouble walking. He used his free arm to hold a sword poised at Tatelyn's back.

"I'm taking these two to better quarters," Elrit said, making his voice lower and gruffer. "It's not appropriate for them to be locked up with the likes of that Elrit." Tatelyn bit the insides of her cheeks to keep from laughing.

"Where's Britaw?" asked one of the other guards, lowering his sword so Elrit could pass.

"Guarding Elrit. That half-elf's a violent one." Elrit nodded and walked Tatelyn and Ramma past the last of the guards. Tatelyn was very glad that Rogan had put the wagon nearer the wild grove of trees rather than overlooking the sea. It would make it hard for the guards to keep them within sight. They hurried to a thicket at the edge of camp and hid behind it, planning their next move.

Elrit whipped off the helmet and took deep gulps of air. "Those things are so HOT," he complained. "Don't the knights' brains bake?"

"I swear that's exactly what happened to many knights I know," Ramma said, rubbing the red marks on her wrists.

"Enough," Tatelyn said, glancing in the direction of the tunnel. There was a handful of guards about the entrance. "How do we get past them?"

"I don't think that trick will work again," Elrit said. "Taking you out of the wagon is one thing. Taking you to the dragon is something else entirely."

"Leave this to me," Ramma said. "Just follow my lead and don't look directly at me." Ramma turned on her heel and strode toward the tunnel.

Tatelyn and Elrit followed. As they neared the tunnel, the guards did indeed look up at them. One of them opened his mouth, probably to raise the alarm, but no sound came out. Each guard looked at them intently, but not one made a motion toward them or even called.

Ramma walked toward the guards with her head held high. Out of the corner of her eye, Tatelyn saw that Ramma's hands were moving swiftly in patterns as she repeated *"Pesona, pesona"* under her breath until it almost sounded like a poem. Keeping her hands moving, Ramma approached the highest-ranking knight and gave him her haughtiest stare.

"I wish to see the dragons," she said, looking the knight in the eye. "So does the founder of the Heirs of Huma and our escort. You shall allow us to pass. You shall not raise the alarm once we are out of sight. You shall forget that we have been here at all. Nod if you understand and will obey."

The guards' heads all bobbed. Tatelyn would have giggled, but that surely would have broken the spell. Without any further words and still keeping up the repetitive hand motions, Ramma strode past the guards and into the tunnel. Elrit and Tatelyn followed her. When they turned a corner out of sight from the guards, all three collapsed against the cool stone wall in relief.

"Where did you learn to do *that?*" Tatelyn asked. Ramma looked drained and triumphant at the same time.

"Don't you have to be a very high mage to control that many people?" Elrit asked.

"That was two parts magic, and one part my mother," Ramma said, rubbing her hands against her skirts.

"Your mother taught you how to do that?" Elrit scoffed.

"You'd be surprised what people will let you do if you act like you have the right to do it." Ramma grinned.

"Wonderful." Elrit rolled his eyes. "Just what the world needs: a wizard with a lady's attitude."

The three of them crept down the tunnel. As they walked deeper and deeper, they heard a soft sighing.

"Wind?" Ramma asked, frowning.

"It sounds more like breathing," Elrit said.

"So what should we do when we reach them?" Elrit asked. "Ramma, can you control the guards down there?"

"I might," Ramma said. "They're not the problem. There's at least one wizard, probably more powerful than me. That's probably how they're able to control the dragons. Brute force couldn't do it alone."

"Still," Tatelyn said, "if we can get to Simle, we might be able to free her father. If we can protect Simle's mother while they fight, we might be able to escape or drive them off."

"It's worth trying," Elrit said. "Let's go!" They rounded a corner and came face-to face-with Rogan, sword pointed directly at Tatelyn's heart.

"Greetings again, sister!"

Chapter Twenty-Two

After her father fell asleep, Simle curled up on the floor and closed her eyes. She didn't sleep, but listened to the people around her. They said little, so all she heard was the clink of weapons, the whisper of clothing, and the heavy breathing of her parents. After a time, she began to hear different noises, noises that seemed familiar.

Tatelyn! That was her voice! Simle's heart lightened, but she kept her head down and eyes shut. The girl must have found a way to escape.

Or, said the cynical part of Simle's brain, she figured out a way to break the spell and is coming back to take your head, or Father's, or Mother's. She could have been planning this all along. Humans are clever.

Yes, they are clever, Simle thought. But Tatelyn wouldn't do that.

Why?

Because . . . because . . . . Simle tried to think of

reasons. Why would the human girl, who hated dragons with such passion, help me?

She wouldn't, scoffed the inner voice. She hates dragons as much as you hate humans.

But I don't hate humans anymore, Simle thought suddenly. Tatelyn is my friend, she realized with surprise. And I am hers. She'll help me because I would do the same for her.

Simle opened her eyes the tiniest crack and saw a pair of violet eyes peering around the edge of the tunnel. Tatelyn! She had come back! She wouldn't be hiding if she were in league with the Heirs of Huma.

Simle's joy was short lived, however. Moments after spotting Tatelyn, she heard the distinct clank and clatter of more armor. There were knights in the tunnel! Should she warn Tatelyn? Keep silent and perhaps have a chance to fool the knights later? Before Simle could decide, Tatelyn, Ramma, and Elrit were surrounded by Rogan and his knights.

Simle groaned inwardly as Rogan lead Ramma, Tatelyn, and Elrit into the cave. Rogan appeared to be lecturing his sister. "Ramma, how could you help them escape? This is our chance to restore honor to our name. You should have watched them yourself!"

"Rogan, this has gone too far!" Ramma snapped. "It's not honorable to even consider what you're doing to these dragons!"

"Those creatures have no honor," Rogan said.

"Now wait here," Simle said, opening her eyes and drawing herself to her full height. "We were your allies during the war! My mother"—Simle choked on the words, pointing to her mother—"was injured fighting for your kind."

"The dragons have corrupted the knighthood. It won't be the same until the dragons leave. Our uncle was driven to madness because of people who believed that metallic dragons could save us. My father was killed fighting alongside them!" Rogan's eyes blazed. "They believed in preserving the knighthood. The knighthood is falling apart because of dragons! I will restore it to its former glory."

"Driving away the dragons will not help the knighthood," Ramma said, standing tall before her brother. "Our uncle was crazed even before the dragons appeared. Our father died honorably in battle. This does not honor either of them."

"Please, Rogan, let the dragons go," Tatelyn said, bowing her head in what Simle assumed was proper respect for a noble from a commoner. "Any wrong done to us by them has been accidental."

"I should have known you would lose your resolve in the end," Rogan sneered. "You spoke fine words, for a farmer's daughter. The creature has bewitched you, pure and simple."

"You can't kill Simle!" Elrit yelled. "If you do, Tatelyn may die!"

"Only one way to be sure," Rogan mused. In a blur of steel, Rogan drew his sword and slashed Tatelyn across one arm. Simle felt the cut deep in her front leg and roared. Tatelyn cried out, but it was in surprise, not pain.

Rogan stared at Tatelyn's wound, then turned to Simle. "So, it's true," he said. "This could prove most useful, most useful indeed. We won't kill the young one—yet."

Simle's heart chilled at those words. She looked to her parents, but they were both sound asleep, as dead to the world as they had been when her siblings were stolen. It's up to me, this time, me alone, she thought. Then her gaze met Tatelyn's. Tatelyn stood there, holding her bleeding arm, but still standing straight to face Rogan. No, not alone, Simle thought with a smile. Not this time.

Rogan looked beyond Simle to the sleeping forms of her parents. He then turned to Britaw and murmured, "Bring me the dragonlance." Britaw bowed and left immediately, presumably to get what Rogan requested.

"No!" Tatelyn screamed, only to be restrained by more guards as she leaped toward Rogan.

"Rogan, this is not the way!" Ramma cried. "Killing a prisoner? One who poses no threat to us?"

"They're dragons," Rogan said, glaring at his sister. "They pose a greater threat to us than anything else that walks Krynn."

"They will if you start killing them without

provocation," Elrit snapped. "How long do you think it will take the metallic dragons to declare war on the knights once word of this reaches them?"

"Oh, very swiftly," Rogan said, pointing at Simle's father. "I plan on sending the head of that one to the metallic dragons immediately."

Everything vanished in a green rage. With a roar, Simle lunged toward Rogan. But the knight grabbed Tatelyn and held his sword at her throat. Simle cut her leap short and landed just short of Tatelyn.

"You cannot attack me, beast," Rogan grinned. The sword point grazed Tatelyn's throat, drawing a tiny bead of blood. Simle felt a tiny prick of pain on her neck.

"This is madness!" Ramma cried. "Let her go! She's not a fighter. She's a cleric and a woman. The Measure of the Knighthood prohibits—"

"She sought to ally herself with this creature," Rogan said, still holding Tatelyn tight. Simle felt an ache in her front legs from the pressure. "The Measure no longer applies to her."

Intar returned, carrying a long, shining weapon.

"A real dragonlance," Ramma whispered, her face pale. "The only weapon forged to penetrate a dragon's scales. How did you get that, Rogan? Who let you near one?"

Simle locked eyes with Tatelyn. The girl stood motionless against Rogan's gleaming armor. Simle felt cold and realized it was from feeling the metal on Tatelyn's skin.

"I'm sorry," Tatelyn mouthed to Simle. Simle blinked slowly to show that she understood.

Rogan handed Tatelyn to another guard, taking the lance and holding it above his head. "If anyone tries to stop me," he ordered his knights, "kill them." He looked at Ramma. "No matter who they are."

Simle scanned the room. Not all the knights looked as though they were happy with this order. The wizard was frowning, as though something, somewhere in his conscience, was pricking him. The people of Forestedge looked angry to see one of their own treated so. Would they rise up against Rogan? She saw resignation fill the faces of those who were not already obedient. There were too many of them. They wouldn't stand a chance.

Panic that she had never felt swept over Simle. She roared as loud as she could. If only her father would awaken! Surely he would now see these people as a threat that must be fought. But her father and mother remained motionless. Rogan hefted the lance and aimed it at Simle's father. His eyes no longer seemed to see the dragon or anything else before him.

Simle heard a cry of triumph as Tatelyn broke free from the knight who held her and raced toward Simle. She didn't stop at Simle, but ran on to Simle's father and placed herself between the large Bronze and the lance, staring defiantly at Rogan.

Rogan advanced with the lance until it touched Tatelyn's breast, just above the Starjewel. Simle felt the sharp pressure on her own breastbone. Tatelyn flinched, but she didn't move.

"You will not kill this creature without killing me," Tatelyn said, her violet eyes flashing.

Rogan tightened his grip on the lance and prepared to send it to its mark.

Tatelyn shuddered violently, and then light flashed in every color of the rainbow as a loud boom shook rocks from the cave ceiling.

Simle gasped and a small bolt of lightning flew from her mouth across the cave. More rocks rained down and the humans ran for cover.

Rogan and Tatelyn remained where they stood, one at each end of the lance. Tatelyn smiled triumphantly, glanced at Simle, then swiftly reached for her medallion of Mishakal, her lips moving in a silent prayer. Rogan slumped to the floor, the lance falling from his hands and clattering harmlessly on the rocks.

Tatelyn and Simle stared at each other across the cave, forgetting all the others. With a quick smile, each turned to fight the nearest guard.

CHAPTER TWENTY-THREE

The instant the last word of her prayer left Tatelyn's lips, Rogan's lance wavered. He staggered back and crumpled to the ground. For a moment, Tatelyn was sure Rogan had been struck dead where he stood. After a moment, however, she saw his lips quiver with an exhaled breath. He was alive after all, and snoring too.

A loud clang resounded through the cave as Simle strained against her chains and broke them. The guards looked from the dragon to their fallen leader.

"We must destroy the beast!" shouted the knight who had brought the dragonlance. He drew his sword and advanced toward Simle.

"Enough!" shouted Tatelyn. "I am leader of the Heirs of Huma! Rogan doesn't give any orders. Listen to me!"

All attention turned to Tatelyn. While she had often spoken to larger crowds, she feared this one more than any she had ever faced. What if she couldn't convince them?

Simle caught Tatelyn's eye and nodded briefly. I have

to convince them, Tatelyn thought. I am responsible for this. I must not let it go any farther.

"My friends, I no longer believe the Heirs of Huma represent a worthy cause," Tatelyn said, her voice ringing thin but clear across the cave. "I spent time in the company of a bronze dragon—a bronze dragon who, by her own account, hated humans as much as I hated dragons."

The Heirs of Huma muttered to themselves. Tatelyn hurried on. "As I spent time with this dragon, I came to discover many things about dragons, and about myself." Tatelyn caught Simle's eye and smiled a lightning-quick smile.

"I had a favorite story that I told when recruiting people to the Heirs of Huma," Tatelyn said. "I would like to share it with you now.

"When Paladine first created the dragons, he made them from metal. They were his beloved children. However, Takhisis stole these dragons and corrupted them. Paladine was so saddened by this loss that he took more precious metals and had Reorx forge the dragons again, the good dragons we know today.

"Once, I told that story to show that if dragons turned evil once, they were likely to do so again." The people began muttering again. Tatelyn held up one hand to silence them. She wondered if anyone else noticed how her hand was shaking.

"I finally know what that story truly means: Paladine grieved for his lost children, but was willing to start anew. He didn't believe that because he lost them before that he shouldn't try again. We all should take that attitude to heart, not just about dragons, but about all creatures.

"That dragon"—Tatelyn pointed to Simle's slumbering father—"refused to fight humans that he considered allies, even when the humans considered him an enemy. And that dragon"—Tatelyn pointed to Simle—"refused to fight because she knew that it would hurt other humans. She knew that any injuries she took would hurt me. A dragon who can't feel pain could be an unstoppable force. But this dragon wouldn't allow even one human to be hurt so she could escape."

Simle looked at the ground and pawed at some of the loose rocks as though embarrassed. Tatelyn saw uncertainty in some eyes, and dawning understanding in others.

"I can't in good conscience continue with the Heirs of Huma. I ask that all of you abandon it as well. There are far greater problems in this world than worrying about potential dangers." Tatelyn then fell silent. She could think of no more to say. Either the Heirs of Huma would believe her and leave Simle and her family in peace, or they would continue their mission.

One by one, every person lowered his or her weapon and, with a final, uncertain glance at the three dragons, walked out of the cave. Ramma glared at the knights who had held her and Elrit, and they hurried from the cavern. Once Tatelyn was sure that none of them were going to attack, Tatelyn ran to Simle.

"The spell broke!" they said at the same time. Simle gasped in surprise and joy and more lightning escaped her mouth and struck the cave ceiling, bringing more rocks down.

"Stop that!" Elrit said as he walked over to them. "We finally get out of this mess and you want to bring the cave down around us?"

"This cave has stood for hundreds of years," Simle said. "When my parents—" Simle stopped short. "Mother!"

Simle ran to her mother in a blur of bronze. She listened to her mother's chest and shook her head. "She's breathing, but I don't know if she'll be all right. It looks like some of the injuries she had before are still there." Simle turned to her father, took his neck in her claws, and began shaking him. "Wake up!"

As Simle tried to wake her father, Tatelyn went to the large female Bronze. It was like seeing a larger version of Simle, but with bigger neck frills. After spending so much time around Simle, Tatelyn thought she had become used to dragons, but here, so close to two fully grown ones, she remembered why she feared them so. Looking at the Bronze, she could once more see the copper dragon flying overhead. Her last words to Brigg echoed in her ears:

"Brigg, look! There's—" Tatelyn *never got a chance to finish that sentence. Stricken with fear, it was all she could do to obey Brigg's last word to her:* "Run!"

Tatelyn remembered hearing about the evil sorceress Asvoria and how she possessed the copper dragon. Tatelyn had never fully understood how any being could be under the control of someone else. But now she knew—it was just like Simle and her. Tatelyn couldn't prevent her own pain. Simle determined whether she felt pain or not, and Tatelyn's actions affected what Simle felt. Asvoria controlled that copper dragon's body—its spirit had gone already. Asvoria could have possessed a bear or a goblin and killed Brigg as easily. It was the person inside the dragon, not the dragon itself.

"Tatelyn!" Simle whimpered, breaking into Tatelyn's thoughts. "Can you help her?"

Tatelyn looked up at Simle's mother. The creature was huge and terrible and powerful. Had she landed in Tatelyn's village, she could have stepped right through the roof of Tatelyn's house and the topmost part of the thatch would not graze her belly. The light in the cave was dim, but the bronze scales still sparkled like purest water. She was the most beautiful sight Tatelyn had ever seen.

Tatelyn raised her hands as high as she could reach and touched the bronze scales. They felt cool at first, then warmed from both Tatelyn's hands and the blood pulsing beneath.

"Mishakal, if this dragon's destiny be not fulfilled, please allow your healing to work through me. Let her be healed."

For what seemed to be an eternity, nothing happened. Tatelyn's heart froze. Had Mishakal answered her prayers about helping them escape, only to deny her the power to heal Simle's mother? Then blue light began to pour from Tatelyn's fingers. It spread up and over Simle's mother like fog over the sea.

"Is it working?" Simle whispered. As if in answer, Simle's mother stretched, nearly knocking Tatelyn over with one outstretched leg. Her mouth opened and a loud yawn escaped, along with a bolt of lightning that landed on Simle's father's back. He jolted awake.

"What? What's happening?" he asked, rising up and shaking his head vigorously. "What happened to all the humans?"

Tatelyn smiled. He sounded exactly like her own father when he first awoke. She kept her eyes on Simle's mother. The dragon was moving and stretching more, but her eyes were still closed. Simle took a step closer.

"Mother?" Simle asked in a low, quivering voice that Tatelyn had never heard from her. Simle's mother's eyelids slowly opened, revealing pupils so wide the eyes appeared to be entirely green. After a moment, her pupils shrank, becoming green dots set in bronze.

"Where's my daughter?" she said in a low, husky voice. "Simle?"

"I'm here, Mother." Simle firmly but gently pushed Tatelyn aside to get closer to her mother.

The dragon slowly smiled. "I was so worried I lost you." Her eyes clouded with acidic tears. "Like my other children."

"I'm here," Simle repeated. She glanced back at Tatelyn and lowered her head. "I was lost for a long time . . . before I left. I know better now."

"Do you?" Simle's mother's eyes focused on the Starjewel hanging about Simle's neck. "So you still have it," she murmured. "Good."

"What is this, Mother?" Simle asked, ignoring her father's sleepy protests for her to stop and let her mother rest. "The human who healed you, Tatelyn, has the other half. Where did you get mine?"

"Humans," the dragon said, peering closer at Tatelyn's jewel. "I met them at the monument to the Silver Dragon— Huma's tomb. There were humans under attack by a black dragon there. I saved them. One of them gave me this."

"I knew that much. Why did you give it to me, though?" Simle said. "Do you know what that gem has put me through? What it put Tatelyn through?"

Simle's mother did not answer, but said, "When I awoke and saw you standing there, I knew the lady was right."

"What lady?" Simle asked. "The one who gave you the pendant?"

"No, not her," Simle's mother said. "After the attack, the humans tried to help me, but I drifted into unconsciousness. I dreamed a lady came to me and told me that the jewel would open my daughter's eyes and to give it to her the moment I saw her. I started home once I awoke, but I met more evil dragons on the way. I couldn't let them harm the humans, so I fought until I could fight no more. Your father found me and brought me home to you. I remember little else until the lady returned to me in my dreams."

"She came back?" Tatelyn asked. "Who was she?"

"She was dressed in blue, like you, my dear," Simle's mother said. "She healed me as I dreamed. She said her name was Mishakal."

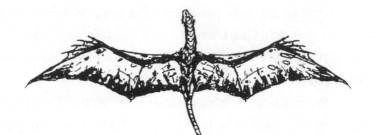

CHAPTER TWENTY-FOUR

One month later, Simle met Tatelyn outside the gates of Palanthas. Tatelyn looked exactly the same in her blue robes, with the medallion of Mishakal and half of the Starjewel around her neck. Simle touched her own Starjewel and smiled.

"You still wear that?" she asked as Tatelyn came closer. "I would think you would fling that as far away as your arm could throw."

"What about you?" Tatelyn asked, grinning. "You could fly to the farthest reaches of Krynn and drop that in the deepest ocean."

"It looks good against my bronze scales," Simle said, coiling her tale about her. "Well? Tell me what happened with Rogan."

"He was going to face a disciplinary council, but Ramma was able to convince them that he was truly mad and would be better at home—locked up." Tatelyn grinned.

Simle giggled. "Glad to hear it. There are no other Heirs of Huma I need to worry about, then?"

Tatelyn looked at the ground and shook her head. "After Rogan revealed himself to be mad and I admitted I was wrong, no one wanted to follow us anyway." She pushed her black braids off her face and looked Simle straight in the eye. "I don't mind—at least, not very much."

"I'm glad. There are other things you could be doing, like coming with me." Simle knelt before Tatelyn. "Climb."

Tatelyn shrank back. "I . . . I can't. I'm supposed to meet with Elistan this afternoon. I'm speaking to a class of acolytes about our adventures. Let my misfortune teach others, Elistan says."

"It won't take long," Simle insisted. "Please, there's something that I want to show you."

Tatelyn wavered. "Can you have me back in time? What if I fall off?"

"Can you trust a bronze dragon?" Simle said, further flattening herself so Tatelyn would not have far to climb.

"Bronze? I though you were copper!" Tatelyn ducked as Simle swung her tail over her head. Laughing, she climbed onto Simle's back. Simle could still feel Tatelyn shaking even once she quit laughing, so her fear of flying must still grip her. Well, there was no better way to get over a fear than by facing it head on.

"Hold tight!" Simle said, then she was running swiftly down the road from the gates of Palanthas.

"Watch out for that wagon!" Tatelyn yelled, gripping Simle tight about the neck.

Simle pushed with her hind legs and they were flying up into the sky. She didn't fly very high so Tatelyn wouldn't feel sick, but rather skimmed about the length of an adult dragon above the ground.

"Are we there yet?" Tatelyn asked above the wind. "I'm not looking."

"Open your eyes, silly girl!" Simle said. "Or I'll plunk you down right now and you can walk the rest of the way."

Simle felt, rather than heard, Tatelyn's gasp. "It's so beautiful," the girl cried. "No wonder you missed flying!"

Simle gazed at the land. She had missed flying, and now took to the skies as often as she could. She circled lazily back over Palanthas so Tatelyn could see.

"Everything is so perfect," Tatelyn said, leaning over Simle's neck so she could see better. "Look at the circles the roads and buildings make!" She then looked up ahead. "And the mountains! I can see so much farther from here!"

Simle followed the coastline to her home, then landed slowly so as not to jar Tatelyn. The girl hopped off almost as soon as Simle's feet touched the ground.

"That was amazing!" Tatelyn skipped around Simle's side and gave her a hug around one leg. "Thank you!"

"No," Simle said, lowering her head and resting it lightly on Tatelyn's head. "Thank you for coming."

"Why did you want me to come back here?" Tatelyn asked. "Your mother isn't hurt again, is she?"

"No, not at all," Simle said. "We're having a special ceremony today and I wanted you to attend."

"Just me?" Tatelyn asked.

"Just you," Simle said. "I like Elrit and Ramma, but this is something that I only wanted to share with my closest friend."

Tatelyn opened her mouth as if to speak, but Simle motioned for her to be quiet. This was to be a silent event. They walked up to the topmost part of the mountain, where the trees' limbs grew only on one side because of the strong winds. Here, the rocks were white and sparkled in the sunlight. Tatelyn turned about in all directions.

"You can see everything up here," she said. "It's almost as good as flying."

"That's why we chose this spot," called Mother. Simle's parents flew above them, blotting out the sun. In slow, lazy circles, they landed before Simle and Tatelyn.

"Where is Uncle Nuvar?" Simle asked. "He was supposed to be here."

"Here! I'm here!" Uncle Nuvar, in human form, ran

up the hill, puffing heavily. He leaned against a rock and wiped his forehead. Tatelyn looked at him, amused.

"You could have flown here," she said. "Why take a human form?"

"So you wouldn't be lonely, my dear," he said, bowing to her. "Simle's parents wanted to be in their natural form for this. And Simle has yet to master transforming into a human."

"You, a human?" Tatelyn turned to Simle and looked the dragon up and down. "Now that would be a sight to behold."

"Well, I already know what it feels like to be human, at least partly," Simle said. "Now I just need to learn how to look like one."

"You two can talk later," Simle's mother said. She then spoke a few words of magic and there was a bright bronze flash that momentarily blinded everyone.

When Simle's dazzled eyes returned to normal, she saw that Tatelyn was standing in the middle of a circle of small dragons. She gasped, not in fright, but in surprise. As her eyes adjusted, she realized that the dragons weren't moving. They were delicately carved bronze statues.

Simle bent her head down to the statues. These were the most realistic statues she had ever seen. She expected them to move at any moment. They all were in different positions doing different things: sleeping, jumping, trying to fly, eating, playing. The only thing that made them different from Simle and her parents were the eyes—there was no life in them.

"These are our children that were lost," said Simle's father. Simle's mother, Uncle Nuvar, and Simle looked skyward. Tatelyn followed suit. "We place these statues here in memory of them." Simle's father inhaled sharply. "We do not know their fate. They may have perished either in an attempt to make draconians or as draconians in the war. They may still walk this land, but are lost to us forever. Wherever they may be, we ask that the Platinum Dragon guard them forever more."

Simle's eyes stung. She moved away from Tatelyn so her tears wouldn't hurt her. When they slowed, she moved back so she could lay her head lightly on top of Tatelyn's.

"I never got to know them," Simle said, her jaw moving Tatelyn's head up and down as she spoke. "Now I know I never will."

Tatelyn ducked out from under Simle's head and turned to face her. "I'm so sorry. Is there no way for them to be reclaimed if they're alive?"

Simle's father shook his head sadly. "The good dragons tried to find a way. I even heard rumors of dragons who trapped some draconians and tried to use magic to change them back. It failed, and they were forced to kill their own children. The only way they would be saved would be if the demons from the Abyss who the black robe wizards called up didn't join with the eggs, which I've only heard of once in the history of draconians."

"How sad," Tatelyn murmured, laying a hand on the statue of the sleeping bronze wyrmling. Simle knew that Tatelyn was thinking of her brother, killed by a copper dragon. Simle's siblings were stolen and corrupted. Which fate was worse? Whose pain was worse? Simle looked at Tatelyn and her parents' sorrowful faces and decided it didn't matter.

Epilogue

Simle spread her wings flat and slowly spiraled down into the garden in front of the temple. Tatelyn thought she and Simle must look like the little seed pods from oak trees in the fall. The workman on the newest part of the temple looked up but seemed to think that a bronze dragon, especially one so young, was no cause for alarm. Clerics on the ground looked up as Simle's shadow fell across them, then scuttled away like ants fleeing a drop of rain. Simle landed lightly and Tatelyn hopped to the ground.

An aged cleric in white robes walked over to them. Tatelyn glanced at him, did a double take, then bowed deeply.

"Who is it?" Simle whispered to Tatelyn.

"Elistan!" was all Tatelyn had time to say before the cleric reached them.

Simle lowered her head in a bow to the cleric. "I have heard much of you, Revered Son," she said.

"And I you, Simle," Elistan said, smiling. "I see you still wear the pendant."

Simle peered closely at the man's face. "Did you know what this would do?"

"I hoped that it would allow Tatelyn to somehow experience, if only partly, what being a dragon is like," Elistan said, looking up at Simle. "It's hard to hate a thing once you truly know it. Only once you both saw the good in the other, and were willing to sacrifice yourselves to save what you once hated, would you be free."

"Is this going to happen again?" Tatelyn asked. Simle jumped. She had not considered that. While she no longer hated Tatelyn, she didn't want the enchantment to come back!

"I doubt it. The jewels have served their purpose." Elistan held out his hand. Tatelyn lifted the chain over her head, removed the Starjewel, and dropped it into Elistan's hand. Simle ducked her head swiftly and her necklace fell into his hand as well. Elistan fitted the two halves of the Starjewel together. There was a blinding flash of light and Simle thought, Oh, no, not again!

When the light died away, Simle bit her tongue and felt relief along with the pain. The Starjewel now shone brightly, all tarnish gone from the silver setting. Elistan held it up so all could see.

"There are clerics traveling to the monument of the

Silver Dragon sometime soon," Elistan said, turning the Starjewel back and forth so it caught the light. "I think they should take these there, don't you agree?"

The monument did sound like a proper place to Simle. Elistan folded his hand over the jewels and rose. He turned to the temple, but then looked back at them. "You know, I always did like the name 'Heirs of Huma.' I wonder if there might be some way to use it in a way that Huma would have truly approved."

Tatelyn and Simle looked at each other, considering.

"A Bronze!" The call rang through the village of Mountainhome during the first light of dawn. Normally, the villagers would just be starting to stir. Now, though, the entire village was up and about as though it were midday. All of them looked skyward at the dragon gliding down at the edge of town.

A group ran to meet the dragon as its feet touched the ground. They surrounded the dragon and immediately began speaking all at once.

"Where have you been?" Tatelyn asked, putting an arm around Simle's leg and pulling her. "I thought you were going to miss this!"

"I'm coming, quit tugging me!" Simle began walking

with the humans at a leisurely pace that matched the hurried stride of the people. "I was recruiting some dragons. It's hard convincing some of them that humans and elves are worth working with. They don't mind protecting them, but working with them?" Simle shook her head.

Elrit snickered behind Simle. "I have heard that those bronze dragons in particular are stubborn."

"That's the copper dragons, not bronze," Simle huffled, smacking Elrit in the head with her tail. "Can't you tell us apart? Honestly!"

"Enough, you two!" Ramma said, lifting her nose out of a book on dragon physiology. "This is very serious business."

"Ah, that's where you are wrong, wizard," Molot said. "This is neither serious nor business to Mountainhome. Look!"

They all halted on the steep trail and looked down upon the village. The sun now shone fully on the houses and every threshold and window was decorated with streamers of bright colors. Mountainhome had little gold, as it was generally considered worthless, but the few items in the village had been twined into a large windchime that hung from the highest fence pole.

"They're preparing for the festivities, once they know all is well," Molot said, leading them into the cave under the barn.

"Hurry!" said one of the guards as they approached. "We may need your help!"

"That's what the Heirs of Huma do!" Tatelyn said, stepping lightly into the cave. Molot held a finger to his lips and they all fell silent. A thin sound like ice breaking shattered the quiet, then another. A hairline crack ran across the surface of a large golden egg. Tatelyn's violet eyes, shining with joy in the light of the fire, met Simle's bronze eyes. They smiled at each other, then watched the first golden dragon to hatch in over a thousand years emerge from the egg.

ABOUT THE AUTHOR

R.D. HENHAM is a scribe in the great library of Palanthas. In the course of transcribing stories of legendary dragons, the author felt a gap existed in the story of the everydragon: ordinary dragons who end up doing extraordinary things. With the help of Sindri Suncatcher and fellow scribes, R.D. has filled that gap with these books.

AMIE ROSE ROTRUCK holds a Master of Arts in Children's Literature from Hollins University where she focused on children's fantasy. She is currently continuing her studies at Hollins towards a Master of Fine Arts. For her day job, she is an engineering manager at a small industrial controls company. When she's not writing, she reads, hikes, works on various crafts, and updates her blog at www.amieroserotruck.com. Amie lives in Maryland with one greyhound, one husband, twenty plants, one hundred dragons, and too many books to even begin to count. *Bronze Dragon Codex* is her first novel.

Acknowledgements

Writing a book is never a solitary process. I was helped along the way by many people who taught, critiqued, or supported me and I am thankful for every one of them.

My mom was my first English teacher and editor. I would not be the writer I am today without her. My dad always encourages my dreams and respects my writing.

There are too many teachers to thank here, but I must single out Dr. C.W. "Chip" Sullivan III, who not only teaches the best classes on the fantastic in children's literature, but also introduced me to the person who would eventually become my editor. Speaking of my editor, I cannot begin to thank Stacy Whitman enough. She is an amazing editor and teacher and I have enjoyed working with her so much on this project! Her editing has made me a better writer and I will always be grateful. Thank you, Margaret Weis and Tracy Hickman, for creating the world of Krynn. While reading about it as a kid, I never dreamed that my first published work would be set there. And of course, R.D. Henham, who had the vision to write about the everydragon. I am especially grateful for my critique group, who whipped through the entire manuscript's first draft in record time. Thank you, Ann Philips, Carlee Hallman, Carol Purcell, Marjory Bancroft, Mary Rose Janya, and Stephanie Lawson for all your input, help, and support!

Special thanks to my fellow fantasy-loving friends, especially those who know why there is a kobold fight in this book.

Last but not least, I must thank my husband, Brian, who had to plan a wedding with someone who was not always in this world. Thanks for everything, and just remember: Never ask a writer what she wants for dinner when she's out chasing dragons.

Amie Rose Rotruck
Assistant to R.D. Henham

**What happens when an evil black dragon
becomes your ally?**

Snatched from the street by a young black dragon, Satia seems
destined to end her life as a snack. But her position as a menu
item quickly changes when her black dragon captor runs into
two young red dragons and a wannabe Dragonlord. Always
one step ahead of their pursuers, Satia makes a bargain with
her captor: her life in exchange for her help. But now she must
live up to her end of the bargain.

Find out how she manages to do that in

BLACK
DRAGON CODEX

FINES
5¢ PER DAY
FOR
OVERDUE BOOKS